Twisted Paths

A MARY O'REILLY PARANORMAL MYSTERY

by

Terri Reid

Although a work of fiction, *Twisted Paths* deals with a problem that has become an epidemic in our schools and in our lives: bullying. An unkind word, a cruel joke, a mocking laugh or a whispered lie – all of these pierce the heart and burden the soul. We have no way of knowing the burdens those around us carry. We can't see the insecurities, the pain, the sorrows or the tragedies hidden behind brave smiles and non-committal responses. We truly can't know if our mean comment will be the last straw – the final burden – to cause someone to do something unthinkable.

Stop the epidemic – be kind. Be part of a cure – be loving. Bolster those around you up with supportive words and an understanding and nonjudgmental heart. And if you truly have nothing nice to say – remember the Thumper Rule – "If you can't say something nice, don't say anything at all."

TWISTED PATHS – A MARY O'REILLY
PARANORMAL MYSTERY
by

Terri Reid

Copyright © 2012 by Terri Reid

The author would like to thank all those who have contributed to the creation of this book; Richard Reid, Sarah Reid, Debbie Deutsch, Jan Hinds, Lynn Jankiewicz and Denise Dailey Carpenter.

And especially to the wonderful readers who walk with me through Mary and Bradley's adventures and encourage me along the way. Thank you all!

Prologue

"I hate you!" Hope screamed as she ran up the stairs to her bedroom. "I wish you would all just die."

Her mother, Gloria, hurried after her up the wide oak staircase, her Italian leather pumps creating a slight tapping against the highly-polished surface. Her jewel-laden hand skimmed the handrail as she quickly ascended, and her face wore an oft-practiced look of disappointment and long-suffering.

Opening the bedroom door quietly, she stood in the doorway studying the girl lying face down on the bed. She really didn't know how to cope with a child that was so…so… She paused for a moment, trying to find a word that was not as cruel as the ones that came to mind immediately. Gauche. Yes, gauche, that was the word that described her second-born daughter. She shrugged delicately; well, she didn't know if Hope was first-born or second-born; she couldn't be expected to remember details like that. They were twins. But in her mind Faith would be the first-born, because they were so alike. And Hope, well, Hope would be…the second-born.

Taking a deep breath she pasted a pleasant look on her face and was about to walk to the bed when the light began to flicker. Impatiently, without thinking, she slapped the wall below the switch sharply and the flickering stopped.

Startled, Hope quickly rolled over on her bed and faced her mother. Blotchy red patches highlighted the array of acne that spread from her forehead down her face and onto her neck. Moisture from her tears streaked down her face, from both her eyes and her nose. Her brown-blond frizzy hair had already escaped her barrettes and the wires from her braces had threads of spittle crisscrossing them. Gloria prayed the revulsion she felt in her heart didn't show on her face. How could she have given birth to such a changeling?

"Hope, darling," she cooed as she glided into the girl's large bedroom. "Now, you know Faith didn't mean to make you feel bad."

"Mom, she did mean it," Hope argued. "She means it when she calls me names at school, she means it when she embarrasses me at lunch, and she means it when she dates the boys she knows I like."

"But darling, that's not fair," Gloria said, moving up and sitting on the edge of the bed. "Faith can't help that so many boys are attracted to her. It doesn't mean she encourages them. I had the same problem when I was her age."

Hope sighed and looked at her perfect mother. Of course she had that problem. She could have almost passed for their sister, well, Faith's sister. Her blond hair hung to her shoulders in a soft bob; her skin was flawless and showed no signs of forty-plus years of life. Her petite frame wore the newest styles perfectly and she could have shared any of the clothes from her daughters' closets. Well, Hope amended again, Faith's closet. Her own closet was filled with loose-fitting, extra-large clothing that hid, rather than accentuated her shape.

"Mom, you don't get it," she said. "This isn't by accident. Faith hates me and she loves to torment me. I think she's embarrassed that I'm her twin."

"No, Hope, I'm sure she's not," Gloria argued. "I'm sure she's just going through some rough times of her own. You know the teenage years are filled with all kinds of pitfalls. It's not easy to be as popular as Faith. There is a lot of pressure involved."

Hope closed her eyes and shook her head. This was not going to work. There was no way her mother would ever understand what she was going through. There was no way her mother could know what it was like growing up an ugly duckling in a family filled with swans. She took a deep breath, opened her eyes and gave her mother the smile of reassurance she knew her mother was waiting for. "Thanks, Mom," she said with a false smile. "I feel much better now."

Leaning forward, her mother placed a light kiss on her daughter's forehead. "I'm glad I could help you, darling," she replied. "Now, clean up and come down for dinner. I've had the cook make your favorite, fried chicken. Of course, Faith and I will only be having salads, but there is no reason you shouldn't have your special treats."

Hope's stomach tightened and tears burned behind her eyes. She would not cry again. She would not let her mother see how hurt she was by being excluded, constantly, from her mother's and her sister's elite club. She nodded. "Thanks, Mom, that sounds delicious."

She watched her mother glide across the room, her posture perfect, her clothes softly shifting over her slim figure and her heart dropped. With Faith around as the model of perfection, she would never have her mother's acceptance. She would never be part of the club. She might as well be dead.

When the door closed behind her, Hope rolled back over in her bed. Silent, burning tears soaked her pillow. Visions of Faith and her mother filled her mind. They were always together, always sharing their own secrets, always shopping in their exclusive stores that only carried up to size six. She wondered how their lives would be if she were no longer with them. She wondered if they would even notice if she were gone. She wondered if they would be a little bit relieved that they no longer had the burden of the ugly duckling shadowing their lives.

Four hours later, the house was quiet and the moon shone through panes of leaded glass in the windows, causing moonbeams to reflect on the walls of the bedrooms like specters of light. Gloria Foley turned off the light in the hallway and made her way slowly upstairs to bed. She paused at the doorway of her daughter's bedroom and shook her head. It had been such an emotional day for all of them. She prayed she would have the strength to get them both through these treacherous teenage years.

Slowly turning the knob on the bedroom door, she quietly opened it to check on her sleeping child. Through the narrow opening, she could see the bed was still made and no one was sleeping on it. She opened the door wider and saw the shadow on the far wall and her heart clenched. Screaming, she flung the door open and ran to the figure hanging from the thick electric cord suspended from the ceiling fan. "No," she screamed, as she tried to lift the inert body up to relieve the pressure against her neck. "Nooooooo!"

Chapter One

Clarissa looked around; no one seemed to be watching them. She sat up on her knees and placed her face against her mother's cheek. *Please breathe, Mommy*, she prayed. *Please breathe.*

But as soon as she felt her mother's cold, stiff cheek, she knew the truth. Her mother was dead.

She buried her face against her mother's neck and wept soundlessly. *What can I do now? Where am I supposed to go? Why aren't there any angels?*

A noise startled her and she turned around. The man that stood in front of the bench just stared at her for a moment. Then he looked beyond her and studied her mother for a moment. Finally, he smiled and squatted down, so he could see her face. "Hello Clarissa," he said. "It's so nice to finally meet you."

Clarissa scooted back on the bench, as close to her mother as possible. She wiped the tears from her eyes and took a deep breath. Maybe the man wouldn't realize her mother was dead. "My mom's just asleep," she lied, "so…no one better think about taking anything."

"You've had a pretty rough day, kid, haven't you?" the man asked, and then he shook his head. "Let's be real, you've had a pretty rough life."

Looking around at the bus station, it seemed that they were suddenly alone. There was no one around who would come running if she screamed. Clarissa shook her head. "Are you the bad man?" she asked, her voice shaking.

"Oh, no, Clarissa," he replied. "I'm a friend of your dad's. My name is Mike and I'm your guardian angel."

She studied him carefully. "You don't look like an angel," she countered.

Grinning, he nodded. "Yeah, believe me, I never figured myself for a gig like this either."

"You don't talk like an angel either."

"I tried that 'thee' and 'thou' stuff, but, really, it just didn't come out right. But if it will make you feel better, I can try it again," he said.

He cleared his throat and looked into her eyes. "If thou art Clarissa and because thou hast been faithful in all things, I wouldst that thou wouldst..."

He paused and searched his mind for a moment. "Wouldst that thou wouldst..." he said again. "Awww, hell."

"Angels aren't supposed to say bad words," Clarissa said, as she slid off the bench to join Mike. "Are you new at being an angel?"

"Yeah, I just got my wings a couple of weeks ago," he admitted. "I was pretty surprised when He offered me the job."

"God?" she asked, her eyes widening.

Mike smiled and nodded, placing his hand on her hair and ruffling it. "Yeah, God," he replied. "He's pretty impressed with you."

"Is my mommy with God now?" she asked, wiping a stray tear from her cheek.

"Yeah, sweetie, she's there with him," he said. "She's safe and now we're going to get you safe too."

"Where are we going?"

He pulled out another bus ticket and handed it to her. "We're going home."

Clarissa studied him and then looked down at the ticket. She was just so tired. Tired of trying to be strong. Tired of being afraid. Tired of being cold and hungry and alone.

"I know you're tired," Mike said, watching Clarissa's eyes widen at his remark. "And God knows you're tired. You've been through a lot. If you can just have faith for a little bit longer, things will get better. I promise."

"Faith?" she asked.

"Trusting in God even when things don't seem to be going the right away," he explained. "Accepting things and, you know, going with the flow for a while."

"Is that what my mommy and daddy would want me to do?" she asked, her voice trembling.

"Oh, yes, sweetheart," Mike said. "That is exactly what your mom and dad would want you to do."

She nodded and took a deep breath. She would have faith, she would be brave, for just a little longer, if that's what her parents would want her to do.

Chapter Two

Mary stood in front of her bathroom mirror and stared into it, not really registering the face looking back at her. She took off her earrings and necklace and placed them into the jewelry box on the counter. Her maid of honor dress was hung on the door and she was wearing a short black slip, silk stockings and a garter belt.

Lifting a bottle on the counter, she applied makeup remover to a cotton pad and started removing her eye makeup automatically.

Gary Copper had escaped. He'd killed Thanner. After all they did, he was still a threat.

Sighing, she leaned forward and rested her head against the mirror. Would life ever get back to normal? Then an unexpected giggle escaped her lips. Yeah, right, who would ever describe her life as normal?

Washing her face, she applied moisturizer and pulled her hair out of the band that held it in place. She turned to pick up her pajamas and realized she had left them in her bedroom. She started to grab for a robe and then remembered, she could walk unencumbered into her bedroom. There was no worry that Mike would suddenly appear with his teasing grin and off-color suggestions about what she should be wearing to bed. She placed a hand on her shower door. The last place Mike had left a note for her, a note that had nearly frightened the life out of her.

Exhaling slowly, she leaned back against the counter. She really missed him. She knew he was in a better place, but there was still a hole in her heart. She slipped out of the bathroom and entered her bedroom.

"Now that's what I'm talking about."

She froze in place, not believing what she was seeing. Perched on the corner of her bed, Mike was sitting; his arms wrapped around one knee as he leered at her in his old familiar way. "Mike?"

He grinned. "Yeah, babe, it's me in the flesh," he grinned and shrugged. "Well, okay, not in the flesh."

"But you…you…" she shook her head. "You went to the light."

"They threw me back," he teased.

Covering her mouth with her hand, tears spilled unconstrained down her cheeks. "I can't believe…" she cried. "I mean…"

He got up and hurried to her side. "Hey, don't cry."

She buried her head in his chest and he held her in his arms for a few moments. Suddenly she backed up. "I can feel you," she said.

"Yeah, I got promoted," he explained. "I'm a guardian angel now. So, it comes with perks."

She grinned up at him through her tears. "You're a guardian angel?" she asked, lifting an eyebrow. "Who'd you pay off?"

Laughing, he wiped away her tears. "I just had to drop your name," he said with a tender smile. "Seems like you got a lot of pull up there."

"So, are you my guardian angel?" she asked.

He grinned and shook his head. "No, I don't have enough combat experience for that job. But we are going to be working together."

"What?" she asked, shaking her head.

"As much as it pains me to say this, you need to get dressed," he said.

She looked down at herself and squealed, and then ran into the bathroom to retrieve her robe. "You should have reminded me," she yelled from behind the door as she tightened the belt.

"Hey, I might be an angel, but I'm not stupid," he teased.

Walking back out, covered by a huge terry-cloth robe, she faced him. She placed her hands on her hips and shook her head. She couldn't be angry, she was so glad to see him. "I missed you," she admitted. "I really missed you."

"Yeah, me too, kid," he replied. "Now, get dressed and meet me at the Greyhound Station in downtown Freeport in fifteen minutes. She was asleep when I left, guarded by a little old lady who would take someone out with her knitting needles if they dared disturb her."

"Who?" Mary asked.

"My first charge," he replied. "Mary, I'm bringing Clarissa home."

Chapter Three

"Ian!" Mary yelled, pulling the sweatshirt over her head as she rushed from her bedroom.

Ian, dressed in flannel pajama pants, shaking the sleep from his face, rushed out of his room and met her in the hall. "What the hell...?" He paused and looked at her face. "You've been crying. What is it, Mary darling?"

Mary threw her arms around him and gave him a quick hug. "Mike's back," she exclaimed, jumping back and smiling from ear to ear. "He's back and he's bringing Clarissa with him."

Ian placed his hands gently on her shoulders to hold her in place. "Okay, now," he said, keeping his voice slow and calm. "Obviously you've had a wee bit of a shock and you're going a bit daft. But it's nothing we can't take care of. Why don't you sit a bit and I'll call Bradley."

She nodded. "Yes, we should call Bradley," she repeated. "We can call him from the car."

"Oh, no, darling," he said. "You won't be driving the car in your condition."

She paused and considered him for a moment, biting her lower lip to keep the laughter from bubbling out. "Ian, do you think I've gone over the edge?" she asked.

"Well, ah, I think that might be a wee bit harsh. And we know you've been under a lot of stress lately," he explained slowly. "But I could fix you a nice cuppa tea and we could talk about it."

She lifted her hands and placed them on Ian's shoulders, mimicking his own position. "Ian, darling," she said in her best mock accent. "I'm not a wee bit daft at all. I came out of my bathroom and Mike was sitting on the corner of my bed. He's not a ghost anymore. He's a guardian angel. He's Clarissa's guardian angel and he's got her on a Greyhound bus coming into Freeport in ten minutes."

Comprehension dawned on Ian's face as his smile spread. "He's back?" he asked. "He's really back?"

She nodded eagerly. "We have to meet him in ten minutes," she repeated.

He threw his arms around Mary and hugged her. "Well, then, what are we waiting for?" he asked.

"Well, you really should get dressed," she suggested. "At least put some shoes on."

He looked down at his bare chest and feet and nodded. "Aye, that would be a good idea," he said.

"I'll warm up the car," Mary said. "And I'll call Bradley while I wait."

Ian paused on his way into his room. "Ah, Mary, about Bradley," he said. "Why don't you just ask him to meet us at the station, but don't tell him why. I think we ought to be with him when he hears the news."

13

"You think he might react the way you did?" she asked, one eyebrow raised.

He just grinned. "Be down in a trice," he said before pulling his door closed behind him.

Mary hurried down the stairs, pulled her phone from her pocket and dialed Bradley's number.

"Mary, what's wrong?" Bradley's voice, although sleepy, was filled with concern.

"I'm fine," she replied immediately. "But I need you to meet me at the Greyhound Station on South Street in about ten minutes. I have a lead on a case I'm working on and I need you to be there."

"Which case?" Bradley asked.

"I'll tell you all about it when you get there," she replied, and then after a moment's consideration she added, "Oh, wear your uniform. I might need a little law enforcement reinforcement."

She hung up the phone, grabbed her purse and hurried out to the Roadster. The night was clear and the stars were shining in the evening sky. Mary could hear the soft call of an owl from somewhere in the vicinity. The ground was cold and the grass crunched beneath her feet. It had been almost a year since Clarissa had been in Freeport. She wondered what the little girl would think about finding her real father.

"She has a real father," a voice said from next to her.

Mary jumped and turned. Henry Madison, Clarissa's father, stood next to her.

"How did you...?" she began.

14

He shrugged. "I just knew," he said. "She's back. She's back in town?"

Mary nodded. "She will be, in just a few minutes."

"How is she?"

"I don't know," she replied. "I only know that she's coming back on a Greyhound bus and that my friend, Mike, is her guardian angel."

He smiled. "She'd like that, her own angel," he said. "I used to tell her all about angels."

"Well, I'm sure Mike is nothing like any angel you might have described to her," Mary responded.

"I'd like to see her," Henry said. "I need to see her."

"Yes, you do," she agreed. "But we need to be sure she's safe first. Gary Copper escaped today. We don't know where he is."

Henry quickly looked around. "Is she safe?" he asked.

Mary nodded. "Bradley, Ian and I will be meeting her at the bus station," she said. "We'll keep her safe."

"And Becca?" he asked.

Shaking her head slowly, she met his eyes. "I don't know anything about Becca," she said. "I'm guessing she's on the bus too, but I'm not sure."

Henry paused for a moment, seeming to search the night air and then he turned back to Mary. "No, she's not on the bus, Mary," he said sadly. "But she's watching over Clarissa just the same."

"Oh, I'm so sorry," Mary said, her heart breaking for the little girl who'd lost so much in her young life.

Ian hurried out of the house and down the steps. He was nearly to Mary before he saw Henry. "Ah, so you've heard the news?" he asked.

Henry nodded and then began to fade. "Bring her to me, when it's safe," he said to Mary.

Mary nodded and waited until he was gone.

"So, what was that all about?" Ian asked as they hurried to get into the car.

"He knew," she said. "He knew Clarissa was coming back to Freeport."

"That doesn't surprise me," he said. "I think our psychic connection with the people we love is the strongest bond we have. I'm guessing that without the physical and mental limitations we place on our own abilities, it's even stronger."

Mary turned on the car and backed out of the driveway. "What do you mean limitations?" she asked, as she shifted gears and drove the car down the street.

"When you tell yourself you can't do something and you believe it, you generally can't do it," he said.

"Isn't that just wisdom?" she asked.

"Could be. Or it could be fear holding you back," he said. "Why can some people see ghosts and others not?"

"Because we have a gift."

16

"Or because they don't want to see a ghost," he supplied. "They don't want to know, so they can't."

"So, Henry can feel Clarissa's presence because he thinks he can?" she asked.

"No, Henry can feel Clarissa's presence because he's opened himself up to the possibility of being able to. He knows he can do it, so he can," Ian replied.

"He has faith," Mary countered, as she turned right onto Empire Street.

Ian smiled. "Aye, faith," he said. "It can do miraculous things."

"So, changing the subject," Mary said with a quick glance over at him. "Why didn't you want me to tell Bradley about Clarissa?"

"Well, first, I didn't want him jumping in his squad car, rushing down the highway to meet the bus and getting her off of it," he said.

Nodding, Mary agreed. "Yes, I could see him doing that. And…"

"And she just lost her father a year ago, the only father she's known," he said.

"And if Henry is right, she's lost her mother too," Mary added.

"Ah, the poor wee bairn," Ian said sadly. "So much for her to deal with. Perhaps she doesn't need to have one more thing, one more major change thrown at her."

"Maybe she doesn't or shouldn't know that Bradley is her father?" Mary asked.

"At least not yet," Ian said. "She might just need familiar surroundings, people she knows, a place to feel safe and a place to grieve."

"It's late, but I'm sure Katie won't mind a phone call," Mary said.

Ian smiled. "Aye, the Brennans would be the perfect place for her to stay for a while," he said. "And it's a place where Gary Copper would not think to look."

"Do you think he's looking for her?" she asked.

He turned to look out the window for a moment – at the dark, quiet houses and the empty silent streets. Then he turned back to face her. "No, Mary, I don't think he's looking for her just yet," he said softly. "I think he'll be looking for you first."

Mary's hands tightened on the steering wheel for a moment and she felt a sick feeling in her stomach. But Ian's words had not surprised her. She had known that Gary would seek her out first. She had escaped him. She had denied him. And she had challenged him. "I know," she whispered.

He placed his hand over one of hers and gave it a quick squeeze. "Aye, and you also know that you will win," he said with confidence, "because you have faith in your abilities."

She smiled. "Faith, it all comes down to faith."

Chapter Four

The squad car arrived only a few minutes after Mary had pulled into the parking lot of the hotel just off Highway 20 on South Street. Bradley, dressed in his uniform, met Mary and Ian in the front lobby. "So, what's going on?" he asked.

"I had a visitor tonight..." Mary started.

"Copper? Did Copper come to your house?" he interrupted.

She placed a hand on his shoulder and shook her head. "No, Bradley, it was Mike. Mike came to me."

"But he went to the light, right?"

She nodded. "Yes, he did," she answered, with a smile on her face. "But he told me he got reassigned; he's a guardian angel now."

Bradley leaned back against the wall and shook his head. "Well, what do you know," he said, smiling back at her. "That's great. That's just great."

"Aye, and for his first assignment, he has quite a special charge," Ian inserted.

Bradley looked at Ian and then Mary. "Okay, who is Mike's new friend?" he asked.

"Clarissa," Mary replied softly. "He found Clarissa and is bringing her back to Freeport."

"What?" Bradley's eyes were wide with shock. "He has... She's coming... Where is she?"

19

"She's on the bus," Mary said. "She'll be here in about five minutes."

He ran his hand through his hair and started pacing. "What do I say to her? What should I do? I'm not ready." He stopped and looked at Mary and Ian, a smile growing on his face. "I finally have my daughter back."

Another car pulled into the parking lot.

"Who's that?" Bradley asked.

"That's the Brennans' car," Mary said, moving up to Bradley. "I called them and asked them to be here when Clarissa arrived."

"Why?"

"Bradley, we have information that leads us to believe that Becca, her mother, has died too," Ian said. "This little girl has probably gone through more than we can even imagine. I suggested she might need a little time with people who are familiar to her before she finds out she has a father."

"It might be nice for her to get to know you," Mary added. "Before she..."

"Before she realizes that a perfect stranger is the person she has to live with," he finished.

"Aye," Ian said, coming up and patting Bradley on the shoulder. "You want the information to be welcome, and you don't want to overwhelm her just as she arrives."

He nodded and turned away from them, looking out the window. Ian went outside and walked over to the Brennans' car. Mary came over to

Bradley and slipped her hand inside of his. "Hey," she said softly, "are you okay?"

His hand tightened on hers and he nodded. "Yeah, I'm just a little overwhelmed," he said, and then he turned to Mary and pulled her into his arms.

She nestled against his chest and enjoyed the warmth of his embrace. He lowered his head and kissed her next to her ear. "Thank you," he whispered.

She looked up at him. "For what?" she asked.

He slowly lowered his head and tenderly kissed her forehead, "For helping bring my daughter home."

"Our daughter," she corrected with a smile.

"Our daughter," he said softly, his face beaming with joy. "We are going out there to meet our daughter."

Taking a deep shuddering breath to keep the tears at bay, she nodded. "Yes. Yes we are."

The bus pulled in front of the hotel and the air brakes hissed to a stop. The door opened and Bradley stepped forward, but paused long enough for Katie to enter the bus before him. "Bradley, I can't imagine…" she began.

He placed his hand on her shoulder and nodded. "It's okay."

She moved down the narrow aisle with Bradley following directly behind her. Toward the middle of the bus, next to a window seat, Clarissa lay curled up and sound asleep. The elderly woman seated next to her looked up at Katie with suspicion. "You know this little girl?" she asked.

Katie nodded. "Yes, I was a friend of her mother," she replied. "She just recently passed away."

The woman's eyes softened. "Well, I'm sorry to hear that," she said. "And who you got with you?"

The woman peered over Katie's shoulder to Bradley. "This is Police Chief Bradley Alden," Katie answered. "I asked him to meet the bus too, to make sure there were no misunderstandings."

"Well, if you've got the Police Chief with you, I guess I'll let you take her with you," the woman replied, pulling herself up and moving out of their way.

Katie smiled. "Thank you."

She started to move forward, but stopped and looked at Bradley watching his daughter sleep. She would have had to have been blind not to see the longing and the love in his face. "Bradley, I was wondering if you would carry her off the bus," she suggested. "It would be easier for you to maneuver her."

The gratitude in his smile confirmed her decision was right. "I'd…" his voice choked and he cleared it softly. "I'd be happy to."

Katie leaned over and gently shook Clarissa's shoulder. "Clarissa, sweetheart, you need to wake up now," she said.

Clarissa sighed and readjusted herself, but didn't open her eyes.

"Sweetheart, I know you're tired, but I just need you to wake up for a moment," she insisted.

Eyes slowly blinking open, Clarissa stared sleepily at Katie. "Mrs. Brennan? Is Maggie here?" she asked.

"No darling, Maggie's at home, still asleep," she replied. "But I thought I'd bring you home with me, so you can spend the night."

A sleepy smile spread across her face and she nodded. "I'd like that," she said. "I missed Maggie."

"And she missed you, sweetheart," Katie said. "I'm going to have my friend pick you up and carry you. Okay?"

Clarissa looked up to Bradley and smiled. "Is he a real policeman?" she asked.

Katie nodded. "Yes, he is," she answered. "He's the Chief of Police."

Still studying Bradley, she finally seemed to accept him. "He looks nice," she decided.

Tears filled Katie's eyes and she blinked them away. "Oh, he is nice," she said. "He is very nice."

She moved to the side and let Bradley get closer. "Hi, Clarissa," he whispered, bending over her. "Welcome home."

She slipped her arms around his neck and allowed him to lift her up. She laid her head on his chest and snuggled against him and his heart nearly broke from the sweet pain of holding his daughter for the first time, but not being able to tell her he was her father.

She sighed. "I'm pretty tired," she confessed.

23

He placed a soft kiss on the top of her head. "I just bet you are, sweetheart," he said. "We'll get you into a nice soft bed soon." .

She yawned widely and nodded, rubbing her head on his shoulder. "Don't forget my backpack," she whispered.

Katie reached forward and picked it up. "I have it," she said and she moved past them to the front of the bus.

Suddenly Clarissa's eyes opened and she looked up at Bradley. "Where's Mike?"

Bradley looked out through the front window of the bus and saw Mike standing next to Mary, smiling at him. "He's here," Bradley said. "He's waiting right outside the bus."

"You can see angels?" Clarissa whispered to him.

Nodding, Bradley smiled down at her. "Well, I can see Mike because he's a special angel," he replied.

"My daddy told me that only good people can see angels," she said confidently, following it with another yawn. "So you must be a good person."

He hugged her to him and slowly walked down the aisle. "I'm trying to be, sweetheart," he replied softly as her eyes closed and she fell back asleep. "I'm trying to be."

Chapter Five

The clock over the mantel clicked loudly in the silent room. It was dark, except for the light coming from the laptop on the desk. Bradley sat in a chair, his chin on his hands, and watched the remote camera view of the Brennans' house. The squad car was situated between the Brennans' house and Mary's house down the street. The officer inside was one of Bradley's most trusted, but he still couldn't bring himself to go to bed.

Holding Clarissa in his arms had changed everything. He was a father. The reality hit him in the gut like a prizefighter's fist. He had a daughter. It was only in the past few months that he learned his daughter was really alive. And it had been only in the past few weeks that he understood that she was within his reach. But holding her, having her cuddle against him, having her trust him... He inhaled sharply. His whole world had been turned upside down.

"Hey, Chief, you trying to peek into Mary's window?"

Bradley whipped around in his seat and found Mike perched on the edge of the couch across the room. He waited a moment, for his heart to resume its normal pattern, and then said, "Man, it's good to see you."

Mike stood and walked toward him. "Yeah, and you don't even need a magic rock in your hand to do it."

Bradley grinned, remembering the trick Mike had played on him a few months earlier. "Well, actually, I put it on a chain and now I wear it around my neck, just in case," he teased.

Laughing, Mike nodded slowly. "Man, it's great to be back."

"It's good to have you back, where you belong."

Mike nodded at him. "Yeah, you know. I said to myself, why hang around in heaven when you can spend your time in Freeport? Especially in the spring, when it's cold, rainy and muddy."

Chuckling, Bradley shook his head. "I always thought there was something a little off with you."

"Hey, watch what you're saying," Mike retorted. "I got a promotion. I'm a guardian angel now."

Bradley leaned back in his chair and closed his eyes for a moment, remembering the little girl he had just held in his arms and trying to control the emotion he felt. "Yeah, Clarissa mentioned that to me."

"So, what did she say?"

He took a deep breath and shrugged. "She said you're pretty new at the job and sometimes you say bad words."

"Well, hell, it's hard to stop," he replied with a grin.

Bradley tried to laugh at his joke, but he couldn't. He just stared at him for a moment and finally said, "I don't know how to thank you, Mike," Bradley said. "You brought my little girl home."

"Hey, don't get all touchy-feely on me," he said casually, but then paused and met Bradley's eyes. "Hey, you're the closest thing to a brother I ever had. How could I not step in? Besides, she's a real sweetheart. She's been through some rough times lately, but she took them all in stride."

"What do you mean rough times?" Bradley asked.

Mike pulled up a chair and sat across from Bradley. "I've been watching Clarissa for a while now," he explained. "Guardian angels mostly have to watch over and not interfere too much. We really aren't supposed to change the consequences of people's choices. But Clarissa didn't make bad choices. She just fell into bad circumstances."

"Tell me about them," Bradley said, leaning forward in the chair. "What happened?"

"Well, first, you need to know that Becca, her mother, is dead."

"What? What happened?"

"Her heart just finally gave out," Mike explained. "She'd been hanging on by a thread for a long time, but she just couldn't do it anymore. That's the only reason I got to come down. Once Becca died, Clarissa was alone and needed a little heavenly intervention."

"Where did you find her?" Bradley asked.

27

"Well, that's a long story."

Bradley glanced over his shoulder at the laptop and saw that everything was quiet. "I've got time."

Mike nodded. "Well, then, get comfortable and I'll fill you in."

Chapter Six

Mary lay in bed, the covers pulled up to her neck, and stared at the alarm clock. Ten minutes until the alarm was set to go off; she hated when she woke up before it went off. Grumbling, she slipped out of the covers, turned off the alarm and headed toward the bathroom. Halfway across the room she paused and instead walked to the window and peeked out. Sure enough, the squad car was still there and it looked like Officer Ashley Deutsch had taken the early shift. She hated to admit it, but knowing the police were watching the house after Gary Copper's escape had helped her sleep better at night.

After a quick shower, she stood in front of her closet deciding what to wear. She and Bradley were going over to the Brennans' for breakfast and then she was going into the office for the day. They had argued about that, but she needed to get back into a normal routine.

Choosing dress slacks and a blouse, she quickly dressed, applied minimal makeup and hurried out of her room, nearly knocking into Ian in the hallway. His hair was sticking out in all directions, his eyes clearly at half-mast and he was leaning against the wall for support.

"Ian, are you okay?" she asked.

"Aye," he mumbled. "I've been up all night doing research about guardian angels. I'd never met one before."

Mary smiled. "And I'd bet you'll never meet one like Mike."

He smiled and nodded sleepily. "And that's a bet I'll never take."

"Why don't you go back to bed," she suggested.

Shaking his head, he yawned. "Oh, no, I can't," he explained. "I promised Bradley I'd be watching over you today, so he can spend the day with Clarissa."

Exasperated, Mary huffed and shook her head. "Ian, I am a fully trained former Chicago police officer. I excelled in self-defense training. I can take care of myself," she explained pointedly.

"Getting a little hot under the collar, are we?" he asked, lifting an eyebrow.

She exhaled slowly. "Yes, I am," she said. "I understand that there's some psychological stuff going on inside me. I get that Gary was able to make me feel vulnerable more than anyone ever has. But how am I supposed to learn to stand on my own two feet again if you and Bradley don't stop babysitting me?"

"We just love you, darling," he explained quietly.

"I know," she said, a little of the steam taken out of her argument. "But I need you to trust me too."

He met her eyes, nodded and turned around.

"Where are you going?" she asked.

"Back to bed," he said with a wink. "You're right. You're a warrior and we need to treat you like one. Can we have lunch together?"

Smiling, she nodded. "Yes, I'd like that," she said. "Sweet dreams, Ian."

"Aye, they will be," he said with another yawn and then closed the bedroom door behind him.

"Obviously I arrived too late today," Mike said, appearing beside her in the hallway.

She jumped, but tried to disguise it. "Too late?" she asked, starting down the stairs.

"To…um…help you decide what to wear today," he said with a wide grin.

"Mike," she chastised, as they entered the kitchen. "You are supposed to be an angel."

He leaned against the counter. "Yeah, well, so I'm an angel. That doesn't mean I'm dead…"

She just stopped and stared at him.

"Okay, yeah, it does mean I'm dead," he relented. "But can't an angel have a little fun?"

"I don't know, Mike," she replied. "Are there angel rules?"

He smiled at her. "More like guidelines."

Laughing, she walked to the refrigerator. "I really have missed you," she said, as she pulled two cans of Diet Pepsi from the shelf.

"Yeah, how much?" he asked.

Walking back, she leaned on the counter next to him and met his eyes. "Every day," she said softly. "I missed you every day."

His smile vanished and he nodded. "Yeah, me too," he said. "Funny, I never realized that when you're dead you still keep your feelings. I'd see something and think, 'Wait until I tell Mary about this...' and then I'd realize I couldn't tell you."

"I kept waiting for you to appear in my bedroom," she said.

"Yeah, well, that can be our little secret," he replied, wagging his eyebrows at her.

"Knock it off," she said, a blush rising on her cheeks. "You know that's not what I meant."

He sighed dramatically. "Yes, I know."

Laughing, she pulled a muffin out of the basket on the counter and wrapped it in a napkin.

"Breakfast to go?" Mike asked.

"No," she replied, shaking her head. "I'm just feeding the officer who's been on duty this morning. I'm walking over to the Brennans' place after that."

"Mind if I join you?"

"It would be my pleasure," she agreed.

After dropping off a can of soda and a muffin to Officer Deutsch, she walked down the street to the Brennans' with Mike at her side.

"So, why the cop?" he asked.

"Gary Copper escaped just before his sentencing," she said. "The authorities are worried he might show up here."

"Is he coming for you or for Clarissa?" Mike asked.

Mary paused before the Brennans' house. "Well, I think we're both at risk. But I don't know if he realizes that Clarissa is here."

"Did I put Clarissa at risk by bringing her here?" he asked.

"No. No, I think she's safer because she has people who will watch over her," Mary said. "And people who understand what Gary Copper is capable of."

"Is she going to Bradley's?" he asked.

"No, we thought about that, but because Bradley could be called out at any time of the day or night and because both Ian and I are at my place, we decided she'd be safer here," she explained. "And the fact that the Brennans are just down the street from me in case of emergency helps too."

Mike glanced at the big house behind him. "Are the Brennans at risk now?"

She nodded. "Yeah, they are. And that's what we have to discuss this morning."

"Well, that ought to be a fun discussion," he replied. "Thanks for including me."

Smiling, she nodded. "Wouldn't want to do this without you."

Chapter Seven

Katie Brennan opened the door, wearing her bathrobe, her hair still in disarray from her short night's sleep. "Do you people ever sleep?" she asked with a yawn.

"I'm so sorry, Katie," Mary said. "But we wanted to speak with you before the children woke up."

Katie nodded wordlessly and led Mary and Mike back into the kitchen. "I understand," she said, "and it makes sense. But it doesn't mean I have to like it."

She slipped into a chair next to her husband, Clifford, picked up her cup of tea, took a sip and immediately looked contrite. "I'm sorry," she said. "Would you like a cup…?"

Mary pulled out her can of Diet Pepsi and shook her head. "No, thanks anyway," she said. "I came prepared."

"We've got about fifteen minutes before the kids get up," Clifford said. "So we'd better start talking."

Mary glanced around. "I thought Bradley would be here by now," she said.

Mike moved over by Mary. "Oh, yeah, forgot to tell you," he said. "He got a call and had to go in. He sent me to tell you that."

Mary rolled her eyes and then turned to Katie and Clifford. "Well, I just remembered that Bradley told me he couldn't make it this morning," she said. "Sorry. Forgetful me."

"So, there's a ghost here too?" Clifford asked casually, taking another sip of tea.

"I beg your pardon?" Mary asked.

"A ghost. That's who just told you Bradley wasn't coming, right?"

Nodding slowly, Mary conceded, "Yes, well technically not a ghost, a guardian angel. He's actually Clarissa's guardian angel. He was the one who brought her here last night."

"I wondered how that happened," Katie said. "Good for him."

Mary was amazed at how well Katie and Clifford were reacting to the news. "You're okay with all this?" she asked.

Katie shrugged. "Well, really, we're not totally awake yet," she admitted. "So we're fairly mellow."

Clifford yawned and nodded. "I'll probably react in a couple of hours."

Mary looked at Mike, shrugged, and then turned back to the Brennans. "Do you remember when we first spoke about Clarissa and how her father was probably killed by the dentist who was on trial, Gary Copper?"

Katie nodded. "Yes, I remember."

"Hey, isn't that the guy who was on trial last week?" Clifford asked.

"Yes, that's the one," Mary replied. "He's also the one who escaped just before sentencing. He's dangerous. He killed his lawyer and there's a good chance he's either in Freeport or on his way here."

Clifford sat up straight. "Okay, I'm awake now."

"So, Clarissa is in danger," Katie said.

Mary nodded. "Yes, because he considers her his daughter."

"But he doesn't know she's here," Clifford said.

"That's right," Mary agreed. "He actually would be coming to Freeport for me. He feels there is some unfinished business between us."

"But once he gets here he might learn of Clarissa," Clifford added.

"Exactly," Mary said. "And we don't want to put your family at risk. There was a police car outside your home all last night, so, even though it was highly unlikely that he could find out she was here so quickly, we didn't want to take any chances."

"What do you need us to do?" Katie asked.

Mary wasn't expecting the emotions that almost overwhelmed her at their simple offer of help. They had children to protect. They didn't need to get involved. And yet, here they were, willing to do whatever she asked of them.

Reaching over, she placed her hand over Katie's. "I don't want to do anything that would jeopardize your family," she said firmly. "But I do want Clarissa to have some kind of transition, so she's just not taken by people she doesn't know."

"That seems wise," Clifford agreed. "What kind of transition?"

"Bradley is arranging to take the day off," she said, "which is probably why he's in the office so early this morning. He wanted to spend the day with her, in your company."

"That's a great idea," Katie said. "I'd been thinking about taking Maggie and Clarissa shopping today, so Bradley can come with us."

"Then, if things seem to go well, we'd have Clarissa stay with me tonight," Mary said. "That way the police are only watching one house and your family isn't pulled into this more than they need to be."

"We don't mind being involved," Clifford said.

"I know," Mary replied, smiling at him. "But I want to be sure your family is safe."

A noise on the staircase behind them had them all turning. Two sleepy little girls walked slowly down the stairs. "Mommy," Maggie yawned. "Is it morning…?"

She paused and her eyes widened in surprise. "Mike!" she yelled and ran down the last few steps and, from her parents' perspectives, threw her arms around thin air.

"I missed you so much," she said, her eyes filling with tears.

Mike returned her hug. "I missed you too, sweetheart," he said.

"Hey, how come you know my guardian angel?" Clarissa asked Maggie.

"This is getting too weird for me," Clifford said, standing up from the table and walking to the stairs. "I'm going upstairs to get dressed."

Clarissa ran around Clifford and joined Maggie in front of Mike.

"He was my bestest friend when he was still just a ghost," Maggie explained. "He's your guardian angel now? You're so lucky."

"You know Maggie?" Clarissa asked Mike.

Mike nodded. "Yeah, Maggie and I go way back."

"And do you know Mary?" Maggie asked, grabbing Clarissa's arm and pulling her over to Mary. "She lets me spend the night at her house and she makes cookies and waffles and everything."

Then she bent over and whispered into Clarissa's ear. "And she's getting married 'cause she's in love."

Mary extended her hand to Clarissa. "Hello, Clarissa," she said. "We met last night, but you were pretty tired."

Clarissa took her hand and looked up at her face. "Are you an angel too?" she asked.

"No, she just looks like one," Mike said, winking at Mary.

"No, I'm not an angel. I'm just someone who cares a great deal about you," she replied, "and wanted to find you."

"Was I lost?" she asked.

Mary nodded. "Well, you were lost to some people who loved you a great deal," she said. "But other people who also loved you, made sure you didn't feel lost."

Clarissa looked up at Mike. "You said you knew my daddy. Did you know my daddy, Henry, or my other daddy?"

"I know your other daddy," Mike said.

"Is he a ghost too?" she asked quietly.

Mary shook her head. "No, he's alive and he's been searching for you."

"Can I meet him?" she asked.

There was a quick knock on the door and Bradley poked his head into the house. "Sorry I'm late," he said. "How are things going?"

"Well, speak of the devil," Mike muttered.

All eyes went to Bradley and there was an awkward silence in the room for a moment, no one quite knowing what to do. Stepping into the house, Bradley closed the door behind him. His eyes immediately went to Clarissa. "Good morning, Clarissa," he said quietly. "Did you have a good sleep?"

A thundering sound behind them had the attention now focused on the Brennans' staircase, as the Brennan boys headed downstairs in search of breakfast. Their usual early morning tussles were amplified by the quiet in the room.

"Hey, what's going on?" Andy called from the landing.

"Hush," Maggie called back. "Clarissa is finding out that Bradley's her real dad."

Mary clapped a hand over her mouth and glanced at Katie who was shaking her head in mortification. She turned to Bradley, an apology on her lips, when she froze as Clarissa slowly walked across the room to face him.

Looking down at the little girl, Bradley's heart caught in his throat. She looked so much like Jeannine, yet he could also see himself in her, especially as she studied him with her all too serious eyes. He squatted down in front of her, so they could see each other eye to eye.

"You carried me last night," she finally said.

"Yes, I did," he replied. "I carried you from the bus and then to the Brennans' van."

"You saw my angel. You saw Mike."

"Yeah, your angel and I have been friends for a little while," he agreed.

"Mike told me he was friends with my daddy," she said, her eyes never breaking contact with his.

Bradley nodded and held her eyes for a moment, forcing himself to take things slowly. He couldn't push, couldn't rush; Clarissa needed to take her time, set her own pace in this discovery. He exhaled slowly. "Yes, Mike is very good friends with your daddy," he assured her.

She moved closer and placed her small hand on his chest. Bradley held his breath. She stared into his eyes. "Are you...are you my real daddy?" she whispered hopefully.

He was amazed at how much joy a simple question could bring. Stunned at the emotional impact it was having on him. He tried to speak several times, but his voice seemed to be caught in his throat. His eyes stung and his heart pounded loudly in his chest. Finally, he just nodded in response to her question.

She stepped closer. "Really?" she asked, her eyes wide and hopeful.

"Yes, baby," he finally breathed, "I'm your daddy. And I love you."

Throwing herself against him, she wrapped her arms around his neck and buried her face in his shoulder. He hugged her tightly, inhaling the sweetness of his little girl, his heart bursting with joy. Finally, he looked up and smiled at Mary. "Thank you," he mouthed.

Wiping stray tears from her own cheeks, Mary nodded back at him. "I love you," she mouthed silently.

"Have to admit, they look good together," Mike said to her.

"Yes. Yes, they do," she agreed.

Katie came over, put her arms around Maggie and hugged her tightly.

"How come you're crying, Mom?" Maggie asked.

"Because I love happy endings," she said, kissing Maggie on the top of her head.

"But, Mom, this isn't an ending," Maggie explained. "This is just the beginning."

Chapter Eight

Mary parked the Roadster in front of her office building, took a deep breath and opened the door. She scanned up and down the street, and seeing no one, hurried to the door with her key already in her hand. After unlocking the door and entering the building, she checked to be sure the alarm was still working and then deactivated it before she moved into the room. She still took a few minutes to check the bathroom, the supplies room and the back door to be sure everything was safe. Finally, she dropped her briefcase and purse on her chair, dialed the phone and held it between her ear and her shoulder as she shrugged out of her coat.

"Well, hello again Mary," Bradley said when he answered her call.

"Hi, I'm at the office," she replied. "I checked the alarm and all of the rooms and doors. I'm secure."

"Good girl. Did you lock the front door behind you?"

She rolled her eyes and then walked back to the front door and flipped the lock. "Yes, I am now officially locked in," she said. "And if I didn't love you so much, you would be a little annoying."

"Lucky for me that you do."

Walking back across the room, she went to the small refrigerator and pulled out a Diet Pepsi and popped the can open. "How are you doing?"

"I still feel like I'm dreaming," he admitted. "I called Jeannine's parents and told them about Clarissa."

"Oh, wow, that was quite a wake-up call for them," Mary said. "How did they react?"

"They're in Florida, taking the first vacation they'd had in years," he explained. "They immediately decided they needed to pack and drive to the airport until I suggested that Clarissa might need a little time before she meets everyone. I thought we could get together next week."

"That's a good idea," Mary said. "Clarissa needs to get to know her dad first."

"I can't believe it. My daughter is getting ready to go shopping with me. I get to shop with my daughter."

Mary took a sip of Diet Pepsi and smiled. "Well, we'll see what you say once the three of you hit the mall."

"I can't wait," Bradley said. "Besides, how much could two little girls spend on a shopping spree?"

Laughing, Mary rolled her eyes. "Just be sure to keep your credit card handy," she said. "And let Katie take the lead, she'll let you know if they're taking advantage of your ignorance."

"My ignorance?" he asked, slightly offended.

"You'll see," she replied.

44

"Wait…Mary…what do you mean?"

Mary grinned. "You'll figure it out," she said. "I have confidence in you."

"But Mary…"

"Sorry, Bradley, I've got to go. There are mysteries to solve and ghosts to bust," she laughed.

"Mary…"

"Love you. Bye!"

She hung up the phone and laughed, picturing him sitting in a chair with that slightly panicked look in his eyes, worrying about shopping with Clarissa. Hopefully that will keep him from worrying about her. Yes, this was going to be a good day!

A half hour later her office phone rang.

"O'Reilly Investigations, Mary speaking," Mary paused to listen. "Yes, actually I do investigate paranormal activities, but I'm not part of a paranormal investigation team. I don't use equipment to catch electronic images or sounds. Is that what you're looking for?"

Picking up a pen and sliding her notepad closer to the edge of the desk, she jotted down the woman's name and address. "Sure, I can come out to see you in an hour or so, if that will work for you," she replied and then a smile spread across her lips. "No, it doesn't need to be dark outside. I can do my job in the daytime. Okay, I'll see you in an hour."

She hung up the phone and reached over to turn on her computer. In a few minutes she found the address she'd been given and whistled slowly through her teeth. The house was more like a mansion, sitting on five acres of land. She mentally upgraded it to an estate. The real estate listing showed that it had only been sold a few months prior and had been on the market for quite a long time. She glanced at the clock and wondered if she had enough time to swing by the newspaper before she drove over to meet with her new client.

Grabbing her coat and purse, she hurried out the door to her car. The paper's offices were only two blocks away, she had time for a quick stop and then she'd drive from the paper directly to her appointment. After parking, she entered the building through the front door. The receptionist was new, Mary hadn't seen her before.

"Hi, I was wondering if Jerry Wiley was in?" she asked.

The receptionist snapped a piece of gum in her mouth and rolled her eyes. "Can I ask who wants to see him?" she asked slowly.

"Yes, please tell him Mary O'Reilly is here," she replied.

The sullen eyes of the young woman snapped open. "You're Mary O'Reilly?" the girl asked as she slid her chair back away from the desk.

Mary nodded. "Yes, I am."

"Do you really see ghosts or are you crazy?"

Mary bit back a grin. "I suppose that depends," she said.

"On what?" the girl asked.

"On if you believe in ghosts or not," Jerry Wiley responded from the door that led to the newsroom. "And since I don't, she's a nut."

Mary grinned. "Just don't tell Anna Paxton you don't believe," she said, referring to the dead society columnist who haunted the building, and watched with delight as he turned and looked over his shoulder.

"Anna isn't here," Jerry said firmly.

Mary walked over to him and smiled. "That's only because she's out on the back dock taking a cigarette break," she whispered to him. "So, can we talk?"

He nodded and raised his arm in the direction of his office. "Sure, it's not like I have to get a paper out every day or anything like that," he growled. "You want me to send out for tea and cookies?"

"No, sorry, I really don't have time for that," she replied with a smile.

She sat down in the chair in front of his desk and waited until he sat himself. "So, O'Reilly, to what do I owe the pleasure of your company?" he asked, not trying to mask his irritation.

"What do you know about the Foley mansion?" she asked.

"It's way above my pay grade," he replied. "Hell, it's above my pay grade to be their gardener."

"Someone seems to be able to afford it," she said.

"Yeah, I heard it finally sold," he said, unwrapping a piece of gum and sticking it into his mouth.

Mary glanced at the pile of gum wrappers heaped on his desk and then looked back at him.

"Trying to quit smoking," he explained. "Been chewing this crap for two weeks now."

"Is it working?"

He grinned at her. "I learned I could smoke a cigarette and chew gum at the same time."

She laughed. "Throw in walking at the same time and I will be impressed."

He chuckled. "Funny, O'Reilly, funny. So, the only reason I figured someone like you would be interested in the Foley mansion is that you and our illustrious Chief of Police are looking for a honeymoon cottage of your very own. But I know what his salary is, so you can't afford it. Or some poor misguided soul thinks there's a ghost hanging out there, right?"

Nodding, Mary leaned forward. "Off the record."

She waited for his acknowledgement.

"I got a call from the new owners," she explained. "They've been hearing strange sounds and they want me to check it out. I just want to know what I'm walking into."

"Okay, well, it ain't pretty," he said, leaning back in his chair. "About twenty-ish years ago, you got the Foley family. Dad's a high-powered attorney, the mom's a trophy wife and there's two kids...

daughters…twins. 'Cept even though they're supposed to be identical, not fraternal twins, something happens when they hit their teens. You know puberty ain't kind to most of us. So one of the twins turns out to be a real looker, the other one's an ugly duckling. The story is, the kid decided she couldn't live up to the Foley reputation and figured they'd be better off without her. She hung herself in her bedroom."

Mary shook her head. "Oh, that's awful," she said. "What happened to the rest of the family?"

Jerry scratched his head for a moment, displacing some of the thin strands of his comb-over. "The other twin, I think her name was Faith, was shipped off to some expensive boarding school in Europe somewhere," he said. "She didn't even make it to the funeral. The mom had some kind of breakdown at the funeral. She was never the same. I think she ended up going to some live-in facility. You know, the kind where they serve you your meds in cut crystal glasses."

Mary nodded. "And the dad?"

"He still has his offices here in town," he said. "The surviving twin got her law degree too and she works with him. She's quite a looker. Does a lot of work with teenage suicides."

"That's nice of her," she said.

Jerry shrugged. "Some people, who ain't so nice as you, say that she caused her sister's death. Said she used to like to tease her and make her look bad. So, could be she's nice, could be she's guilty."

"Do you think some people are right?" she asked.

Rubbing the back of his neck, he stared off across his office for a moment. "Funny thing, actually, more woo-woo creepy than funny."

"What?"

"A couple years after her death, one of the girls who used to hang out with the sister killed herself," he said, "on the same date as the first suicide."

Sitting forward on her chair, Mary pulled out a pad of paper and a pen. "That is weird," she said. "What was her name?"

"Mandy…something," he replied. "I'll look it up and send it to you."

"Thanks, I'd really appreciate it."

"Yeah, yeah," he replied absently, not concentrating on Mary's response. "There was something else. Something I should tell you."

She waited.

Finally, he turned back to her. "Something's niggling in the back of my mind," he said. "But I can't put my finger on it. I'll let it percolate for a little while and it'll come to me. I'll send you an e-mail when it does."

Mary stood up. "Thanks, Jerry," she said. "Once again, you're a fount of information."

"Yeah, just remember, you owe me, O'Reilly," he replied as she walked out of his office.

Chapter Nine

Mary was just on time to her appointment. The house looked even more impressive in person than the virtual online tour had shown. She parked her car at the top of the circular drive and walked up the narrow pathway to the house. The door opened before she had a chance to knock.

"Mary O'Reilly?" the young woman asked.

Mary nodded. "Yes, I'm Mary," she replied.

"You don't look like... I was expecting, something, someone different," she said.

Mary smiled. "A turban around my head and a flowing caftan?" she asked.

The woman smiled slightly and nodded. "Something like that, I suppose. Please come in, I'm Faye Vyas."

Yes, it certainly was fancy, Mary thought as she entered the foyer.

Decorated in muted shades of peach, from nearly white to nearly brown, everything in the home suggested the influence of a skilled interior designer. The highlight of the foyer was a large sweeping staircase of polished wood that smelled slightly of lemon polish. It was a nice touch and Mary looked around for a plug-in air freshener, because she knew the woman next to her had never held a polishing rag in her professionally-manicured hand.

51

Unopened boxes sat alongside the staircase and, as she looked through the open doorways from the hall, Mary could see a large number of unopened boxes throughout the house.

"Did you just move in?" Mary asked.

Faye, following Mary's gaze, shrugged and sent her an unrepentant glance. "After the incident, I don't like being here alone," she said, "so we've been living at a hotel since the first week we moved to town. We don't know if we're going to be staying here yet."

Comprehending immediately, Mary nodded. "Other than the ghost, is there a problem with the house?" she asked.

Shaking her head, Faye looked overwhelmed. "No," she said, her voice shaking slightly. "No, I love this house. It's everything I ever wanted. But I can't..."

She clasped her hand over her mouth and took a deep shuddering breath. "I never, ever, believed in things like this," she confessed. "I mean, when you're dead, you're dead. Right?"

Mary shrugged. "Well, unfortunately, not always."

"Can you get rid of it?"

Looking squarely at Faye, Mary shook her head. "You do understand that I'm not an exterminator. I'm not a ghostbuster, like in the movies. If you have a ghost, it's generally because something happened to someone in your home and they haven't found their way to the other side yet."

"Well, can't you hurry them on?" she asked, shooing her hands forward as if Mary could herd the ghost on.

Sighing, Mary nodded. "Well, let's see what I can do. Where does the phenomenon manifest itself?"

"Upstairs, in the bedroom," Faye said, climbing the stairs without waiting to see if Mary would follow.

Jogging up behind her, Mary wondered just how involved her client wanted to be. "When I walk into the bedroom, I will potentially be able to see what happened in there," she said. "Do you want me to tell you what I find?"

Faye stopped at the top of the stairs and faced Mary. "Oh, no, good grief, I don't need those kind of details," she said. "I just need you to tell me if you can make it go away, or cross over, or whatever."

Faye hurried down the hall, pushed open a door and stepped back, allowing Mary to enter.

Mary stepped inside the room. The sun was filtering in through the paned windows, the lace curtains enhanced the view of the countryside, and the light sage colored walls were accented perfectly with the soft gray carpeting. The room had yet to be furnished, but everything was ready and lovely, except for the teenage girl hanging from a thick extension cord from the ceiling fan in the middle of the room.

"Hello?" she said quietly as she approached the ghost. "Can I talk to you? Why are you still here?"

There was no response. Mary understood that this ghost was merely a shadow of an event, not an interactive or intelligent ghost that would be able to speak with her. If there was a chance of contact, it would happen when the ghost was active and reenacting her death. "When do you hear the ghost?" she called out.

"We hear it every night at ten p.m.," Faye called back to her, not entering the room. "Every single night of the week. We hear a shuffling sound, then a door slams shut and then something drops."

Mary thought about Clarissa and Bradley, and knew this mystery was going to have to wait one more day.

"Well, I know what your problem is," Mary said, coming out of the room. "But I won't be able to help you until I can witness the event myself. I can't come back tonight, but I could make it tomorrow night."

"You have to come back? You can't just use some electrical equipment and get rid of it?" she asked.

Mary shook her head. "No, I will have to interact with her and find out what's keeping her here."

"Her? It's a girl?" Faye asked.

Mary nodded. "Yes, a teenage girl. It looks like…"

"Stop," Faye demanded, placing her hands over her ears. "I don't want to hear about it. It will just freak me out. Fine, we'll spend another night at the hotel. You can come back tomorrow night and then, hopefully, you'll be able to fix things."

"Yes, hopefully, I will," Mary replied. "For all of our sakes."

Chapter Ten

Mary drove back to her office, her mind on the list of things she'd need to get ready for dinner that night. She wondered what Clarissa liked to eat. If she was anything like Mary when she was her age, macaroni and cheese and fish sticks would have been a treat. Going through her mental checklist she realized that she'd have to cancel lunch with Ian and run over to the grocery store instead. Maybe she should pick up cookies at Cole's Bakery. *Why, oh, why did Rosie have to choose this week to go on her honeymoon?*

Mary pulled into her parking spot and smiled, thinking of both Rosie and Stanley. *Well, just getting married probably had something to do with it.*

She reached over to the passenger seat to get her purse and froze. The hairs on the back of her neck raised and she knew she was being watched. She slowly turned around and scanned the sidewalk. There, at the end of the street, a man was watching her. Or at least he was watching her office building. She squinted to get a better view. Even though he was wearing an oversized jacket and a hat, she knew it was Gary Copper.

She dropped her purse and slipped out the car. She kept low, behind the parked cars, as she tried to make her way to the corner without being caught.

The traffic was light and no one was walking down the street. She knew surprise was her best defense because even if he had a weapon, he would have to react quickly in order to use it.

Linda Sterling, the County Clerk left her office to run down the street to the Post Office. She walked out into the brisk, sunny day with a smile on her face and when she saw her good friend, Mary, her smile widened. She hadn't seen Mary since the day she was married, when Mary stopped her abusive stepfather from ruining her wedding.

She watched Mary walking behind the cars and shook her head. Mary was always doing something a little weird, but her heart was good. She wondered if Mary had time to stop in at Nine East, the local coffee shop, for a few moments.

Mary was nearly directly across from Gary when Linda called out.

"Mary," she yelled, waving her arm. "Mary over here, do you have a minute?"

Gary's head snapped to attention and he quickly glanced around the area. Mary tried to duck, but their eyes met in the reflection of an SUV. Gary's eyes narrowed and then he turned and ran down the street.

Not wanting to lose him, Mary took off after him. "Linda, call the police," she yelled.

Mary dashed around the corner just in time to see Gary cut through the parking lot and head toward Debate Square.

"Hey, coward, why don't you face me?" she called after him, before she hurried down the steps and dashed between the parked cars. She wished she had her running shoes on, instead of heels, but she was still making pretty good time. She ran across the street, into the small park and through the parking lot behind it. She was only twenty yards behind him.

Turning, he glanced back at her before slipping between two brownstone apartment buildings, knocking trash cans down behind him. Mary leapt over the cans, nearly tumbling when her heel slipped on some garbage, but righted herself and continued the pursuit.

She paused for a moment at the end of the gangway, breathing heavily and looking up and down the alley to see where he'd gone. She saw him turning the corner and heading back to the downtown retail district. Mary continued to run after him, praying that police would get Linda's call and respond immediately, because he could easily get lost in the stores.

Running up State Street, she looked into store windows as she passed them. *Crap! I can't lose him*, she thought.

She ran faster, her lungs nearly exploding as she pushed herself. Finally, on the corner of State and Stephenson, she had to admit that she'd lost him. Jogging down the block to Rite-Way Furniture, she pushed open the door and nearly collapsed. Cal, the owner, hurried from the desk.

"Mary, what's wrong?" he asked.

"Cal, call 911," she breathed heavily. "Tell them Gary Copper's in town. Tell them I lost him in the downtown area."

Pulling his cell phone out of his pocket, he punched in the numbers, while he led Mary over to one of his large recliners. "You sit down and rest," he ordered.

He relayed the information to the dispatcher and then got a bottle of water for Mary. "They're sending someone over here," he explained. "Are you okay?"

Nodding, she leaned back in the chair. "Yeah, thanks," she said. "And thanks for making the call."

"Hey, no problem," he replied. "So that's the guy who escaped in Sycamore, right?"

"Yes, that's him," she said. "He killed his lawyer and somehow got out of the building."

"Sounds dangerous."

"He is," Mary agreed.

"Do we have a photo we can send around through the Freeport Downtown Development Foundation to all the downtown retailers? So, they can make a call if they see him?"

Smiling, she sat up. "That's a brilliant idea," she said. "Thanks, Cal, I'll email one to you as soon as I get back to my office."

"Yeah, well, I don't know if you'll be going back to your office," he said, his gaze going past her to the giant showcase windows in front of the store. "Looks like they called Chief Alden and I got a feeling he's not going to let you go very far from his side until this guy is caught."

Mary flopped back in the recliner and watched as Bradley pushed open the front door and hurried toward her.

"Mary, are you okay?" he asked.

"That man's whipped," Cal whispered.

"Yeah, well, I don't think that's love and kisses in his eyes right now," she said to Cal and then she turned to Bradley to reassure him, "Yes, I'm fine. Just a little upset I lost him."

"What the hell were you thinking going after him by yourself?" he demanded.

She sat up in the chair. "I was pursuing a fugitive," she shot back.

"What if he had a gun?"

"He wouldn't have run."

"Mary," he growled.

"Bradley," she responded. "Don't try to pull rank on me."

He exhaled slowly, ran his hand through his hair and squatted down next to her. "Okay, you're right. But, damn it, I wouldn't want any of my officers pursuing a man like Copper by themselves. You should have called for backup."

She took a deep breath too. "I acted on instinct," she said. "But you're right, I should not have left my cell phone in the car. And I should have called for backup. I'm sorry."

He took her hand in his and looked into her eyes. "You're okay? Really?"

She smiled at him. "Yeah," she said softly. "A little freaked out maybe."

Then her eyes widened. "Who's with Clarissa?"

"She's at the station," he said. "I left her there with Ashley Deutsch. She's safe."

Mary nodded, her heart going back to a normal rate. "It's different now," she said. "Now it's not just us we have to worry about."

Smiling, he squeezed her hand. "Yeah, but it's a different I like."

Chapter Eleven   .

Clarissa was sitting in Bradley's office chair and spinning in it behind the desk, when Mary and Bradley arrived at his office a little while later. Mike was standing in the corner of the room, watching over Clarissa. Officer Ashley Deutsch, sitting across the desk from her working on some reports and totally oblivious to Mike's presence, looked up when they walked in.

"How did it go?" she asked.

"I lost him," Mary replied, shaking her head. "He just disappeared near State and Exchange. I ended up running into Cal's and asked him to phone in."

"Are you sure it was Copper?" Ashley questioned.

Nodding, Mary walked into the room and sat down in a chair near Ashley. "Yeah, I won't ever forget that face."

"So, we've got an APB out on him," Bradley said to Ashley. "But I'd like you to canvas the downtown area with his photo and let the community know this guy is very dangerous."

"Do we need any school lockdowns?" she asked.

"No, I don't think he's a threat to the public at large," Bradley said. "But it wouldn't hurt to send an email to the school district and have them circulate the photo too."

"Cal suggested we send it through the Freeport Downtown Development Foundation and they could send it on to some of the retailers," Mary added. "But you should probably follow up because many of the small mom and pop stores don't have email."

Ashley nodded, gathered up her reports and turned to Clarissa. "So, remember what I told you," she said.

Clarissa grinned and nodded. "I will," she agreed.

"Excellent," Ashley said with a smile and she winked at Clarissa before leaving the room.

"Told you?" Bradley asked, taking Ashley's chair.

"Ashley said if I ever need a babysitter who can shoot a gun, I should call her," Clarissa replied. "She's nice. And brave. But she didn't even know Mike was here."

"That's our little secret," Mike said, coming to join them at the desk. "And you were an exceptional young lady while you waited."

"That's good to hear," Bradley said, stroking Clarissa's head.

"So, how are you doing?" Mike asked Mary.

Clarissa moved her chair so it faced Mary. "Were you chasing the bad man?" she asked.

Mary nodded. "Yes, I was. But, unfortunately, he got away."

"But he ran away, so he was scared of you, right?"

"Right," Mike agreed.

"Well, I don't think he wanted to get caught," she answered. "So, I suppose he was afraid of me."

"So, you're brave, right?"

"Mary is very brave," Bradley inserted, turning to smile at Mary and whispering softly so only she could hear, "and very stubborn."

Clarissa slid off the chair and walked over to Mary. "Maggie said you can see things like she does. Like the sad lady. Did you ever see my birth mommy?"

Nodding, Mary bent at her waist to lean closer to Clarissa. "Yes, I saw your mommy," she replied. "She and I became very good friends and she asked me to help your daddy find you."

The phone rang on Bradley's desk and the conversation halted as Bradley stood up and reached over to pick it up. "Chief Alden."

He paused for a moment. "Hey, Bernie, it's good to hear from you too," he said, looking over to Mary. "Yeah, she's right here. We've had a busy morning."

He listened for a moment, his face sobering and he nodded. "Thank you," he said. "Yes, please send her here to Freeport. I'll take care of the arrangements."

Sighing deeply, he hung up the phone and walked around the desk in front of Clarissa. Squatting down in front of her, he took both of her hands in his.

"Clarissa, sweetheart, the man that called is a friend of mine from Chicago," he said. "He called to tell me that..."

He stopped and exhaled sharply. "Sweetheart, they found your mother, Becca."

"At the bus station?" she asked.

"Yes," he replied. "A policeman found her at the bus station."

"Did he know she was dead?" she asked innocently.

Surprised, Bradley paused for a moment, and then asked, "You knew she was dead?"

Clarissa nodded. "Yes, when I woke up from my nap, she was already dead," she explained. "She wasn't breathing and I knew she went to live with God, just like my daddy Henry."

Mary bit her lip to hold back her tears. "Were you frightened?" she asked.

"Well, I was a little 'cause I looked up and saw a man. I thought it was the bad man," she said. "But it was Mike saving me just like my daddy Henry said he would."

Mike looked down at her. "What did he say?" he asked.

She smiled up at him. "He said God always sends angels just when you need them."

"Yes, he does," Mary said, looking up at Mike with gratitude. "Just when you need them."

Clarissa looked at Bradley. "What is the policeman going to do with my mom?"

"He's going to send her here," Bradley said. "And we'll have a funeral for her and bury her next to your daddy Henry."

She smiled at him. "She'll like that," she said. "She missed him lots."

Mary ran her hand over her eyes to wipe away any stray tears. "Well, I know just the man who can help us plan a nice funeral for her. His name is Mr. Turner," she said. "Should we go over and see him and pick out the flowers for her?"

Nodding, Clarissa turned to Bradley. "Can I?"

He leaned over, picked up her coat from the back of her chair and handed it to her. "Yes, I think that's a great idea and I think we all should go over there," he said.

Chapter Twelve

"Ach, no, you can't do this to me," Ian groaned from the living room. "Please darling, have a little mercy."

Clarissa giggled. "No, I jumped three of your checkers. Now you have to crown me."

"You're naught but a wee grown-up here to fleece me out of my chocolate chip cookies," he replied.

"I'm not a grown-up," she said. "I'm just a little girl. But I would like another cookie."

"Aye, but don't let on that I'm giving you another," he said.

Mary pulled the last dish out of the sink and handed it to Bradley to put in the dishwasher. "Should we let him know we can hear him?" she asked.

Shaking his head, he quickly slipped the dish into the place and closed the door. Then he grabbed Mary's hand and pulled her toward the back door. "No," he whispered. "Let's just pretend we're still busy cleaning things up."

He opened the door and ushered her out onto the back porch.

"Why do you want to pretend…?" Mary began, but her words and her thoughts were cut off as Bradley's lips covered hers.

He pulled her to him, angled his head so he had greater access and deepened the kiss. He inhaled the fragrance of her shampoo as he skimmed his lips over her forehead. The scent was uniquely Mary; cinnamon, vanilla and something spicy. *Delectable,* he thought as he lowered his head to cover her lips again, *perfectly delectable.*

Mary's insides were engaged in a slow steady meltdown and her heart was running a marathon. How did he do this to her with only a kiss? Whatever spell he wove, she was bewitched. Wrapping her arms around him, she slid her hands across the broad planes of his back, feeling the flex of his muscles as he held her and relishing the strength in his arms and the gentleness of his embrace. Had any other woman ever felt so cherished?

The slight stubble on his face rubbed against her cheek and sent a small explosion through her center. His hot breath against her neck caused another. And the way he murmured her name before he crushed his lips against hers took her breath away. She was burning inside, her body tightening to a fevered pitch and she knew he burned just as passionately for her.

Finally, he slipped his lips from hers and just held her, his cheek on the top of her head, his breathing labored. She slid her hands down and wrapped her arms around his waist, resting her head against his shoulder. The sound of his racing heart reassuring her that he was just as disturbed as she.

"I can't wait," she whispered.

He was silent for a moment, and then kissed the top of her head. "For what?" he asked quietly.

"For the day we don't have to stop at kissing," she admitted.

He tightened his hold for a moment, and then released her. His hands slid slowly down her arms as he stepped back and looked down at her, meeting her eyes. She could see the desire, the passion and the hunger. The intensity almost frightened her, but her body shivered in response.

He bent down and kissed her once more, reluctant to end the intimacy. "Soon, darling," he promised, against her lips. "Very soon."

"Uh hum," Mike cleared his throat loudly behind them. "Okay, well, this is awkward."

Mary heard a quiet swear word slip from Bradley's lips and had to bend her head against his chest to hide her smile.

"You needed something?" Bradley asked.

Mike grinned at them. "Well, yeah, sorry and all," he said. "But Clarissa has had a pretty full day and she's just about asleep on her feet in there."

Bradley sighed. "Sorry, Mike, you're right. We'll be in there in a moment," he said.

Mike winked at Mary and then disappeared.

"You can stop smiling now," he said to her.

She giggled. "Sorry," she said raising her face to his. "I don't know what came over me."

He smiled down at her. "I love you, Mary O'Reilly," he said. "That's what came over me."

"I love you too, Bradley Alden," she replied. "Now let's go put our daughter to bed."

Chapter Thirteen

After good-night wishes from all of the men in the house, Mary took Clarissa upstairs to help her get ready for bed.

"Do I get to live here?" Clarissa asked as they entered her bedroom.

"Yes, you do," Mary replied, pulling a new set of pajamas out of the drawers. "Do you think you'll like it?"

Clarissa looked around the room, the walls were pale blue and the woodwork was white. The shelves were nearly empty, with only a few of her possessions lying on them. Her dresser matched her bed, a delicate white enamel-painted set with small appliques of roses on them. There were new toys, still wrapped in their original packaging in a shopping bag from the store and a huge stuffed teddy bear in the middle of her bed.

"My mommy would have liked it," she said sadly. "She loved the color blue."

Mary gave her a hug. "What was her favorite blue thing?" she asked.

"She had blue slippers," Clarissa said, her eyes filling with tears. "Daddy bought them for her for Christmas. She loved them lots."

"Those slippers sound wonderful," Mary said. "And your parents sound like they loved each other very much."

Clarissa nodded. "I miss them."

"Of course you do, darling," Mary replied. "And I'm sure they miss you."

She took a tissue from the dispenser on the table next to the bed and gently wiped Clarissa's face. "They loved you so much," she said.

Taking a deep shuddering breath, Clarissa nodded and remembered what Mike had told her. "I'm trying to have faith," she explained to Mary. "And not be too sad."

"Having faith is sometimes a hard thing to do," Mary said. "And you seem to be doing an exceptional job."

Smiling, Clarissa looked around the room again. "I do like it here, very much," she admitted.

"I'm so glad," Mary said. "Now, through that door is your bathroom. Why don't you wash up and brush your teeth, and I'll try to organize some of your things."

Clarissa walked through the open door, her pajamas in hand, and Mary could hear the water running in the sink. She took some of the toys out of the bag and was walking to the shelf when Henry appeared in front of her. She jumped back and dropped the toys onto the rug. "You could have warned me," she whispered harshly.

"Sorry," Henry said. "I just wanted to be sure she was safe."

"Mary," Clarissa called from the bathroom.

"Yes, sweetheart," Mary called over her shoulder.

"Is my mom with my dad now?" she asked.

Mary looked at Henry and raised an eyebrow. "What would you like me to say to her?" she asked.

"Tell her..." he paused for a moment. "Tell her that her mother and I are together in heaven."

"But I can let her know..." Mary began.

He shook his head.

"Yes, your mom is with your dad now," she said.

Clarissa walked out of the bathroom, dressed in her new flannel nightgown, with a toothbrush in her mouth. "Good," she said, around the scrubbing. "'Cause he always took care of her. Now he can take care of her again."

"Who took care of her when you were in Chicago?" Mary asked.

"Well, I think Mom thought she was taking care of me," she said. "But I took care of her. And now she can just rest."

Henry moved over to Clarissa's side and smiled down at her. "She was always a brave little soldier," he said. "She always did more than she should."

Clarissa hurried back into the bathroom to spit out the toothpaste and rinse her mouth, then she climbed up into her bed. Mary sat down next to her and tucked her in. "How did you take care of your mommy?" she asked.

Shrugging, Clarissa leaned back into the pillows and yawned. "I just took some of the worry away from her," she said, "just like Daddy Henry used to do. We both took the worry away from Mommy."

Mary leaned forward and kissed her forehead. "That was a wonderful thing to do," she said. "And I'm sure your Daddy Henry appreciated it."

Yawning, Clarissa nodded. "We're a team, Daddy Henry and me," she explained, her voice getting softer. "That's what he always said. We were a team."

"Come on, let's get you under the covers," Mary suggested.

Snuggling into the pillow, her eyes heavy, she looked up at Mary. "Can you tell me a story?" she asked. "One about angels?"

Henry moved over to stand next to the bed. "When God created the world he had a plan," he began.

"When God created the world, he had a plan," Mary repeated.

Clarissa's eyes widened. "That's the story Daddy Henry would tell me," she said.

Henry sat down on the other side of the bed. "That all of us would come down to earth and be born."

"That all of us would come down to earth," Mary repeated.

"And be born," Clarissa added.

"Exactly," Mary said, sharing a smile with Henry.

"And the jobs of the mommies and the daddies were to take care of the children so they would learn how to be good, right?" Clarissa said.

"That's right," Mary agreed and then after listening to Henry added, "but God knew that sometimes people would need extra help."

"So he made angels," she yawned, her voice soft with awe. "Just like Mike."

Mike appeared in the corner of the room and nodded at Henry. He moved over to the bottom of the bed. "Yeah, just like me, sweetheart. And just like your Daddy Henry."

"Daddy Henry said angels are all around us," she whispered. "And they are closer than you think."

"Yes, darling," Mary said, stroking Clarissa's hair. "They are often closer than you think."

Her eyes were closing and her breathing was becoming more rhythmic. "I miss my Daddy Henry," she said softly, her voice coming out like a breath.

"He misses you too darling," Henry said, lowering his head to kiss her brow. "He misses you, too."

Chapter Fourteen

Mary sighed as she sat at the kitchen table with her laptop in front of her. She let Bradley talk her into working from home while Gary was still on the loose, but sitting in her house all morning was driving her crazy. Ian was upstairs doing some research and Clarissa was with Bradley at the station for the day.

She got up, put the kettle on for another cup of tea and heard footsteps on the staircase. Ian appeared in the kitchen a moment later. "You wouldna have enough water in that pot for another cuppa would you?" he asked.

"Sure, there's plenty," she replied, and then she reached up to the cabinet. "And if you stay downstairs and actually carry on an adult conversation with me, I'll share my Oreos with you."

He immediately pulled out a kitchen chair and sat down. "And what would we be talking about this fine morning?" he asked with a grin.

She put a number of cookies on a plate and set it before him. "See, I like a man who's easily bribed," she said. "Now why can't I trade Bradley some cookies for my freedom?"

Ian picked up a cookie and bit into it.

"Wait, you don't eat those like that," she objected. "You're supposed to twist the top off and eat the center first."

Ian held the partially consumed cookie in his hand and looked at her inquisitively. "You have rules for how you eat a cookie?" he asked.

Mary shrugged, a little embarrassed. "Well, not all cookies," she explained, "just some cookies."

"Aye, and where would a fellow be finding a handbook that gives you instructions on the whys and wherefores on cookie eating in the States, then?" he asked.

She sighed. "Never mind, just bite it," she said, turning away from him. "I just can't watch."

He grinned at her, then twisted the top off the cookie and held a part in each hand. "And now, what's the next step, oh wise instructor?"

"You scrape the frosting off both sides," she said.

"You don't eat the frosting with the cookie?"

"No, you scrape it off with your teeth and then you eat the two chocolate cookies by themselves."

"Well, then, why don't you just buy unfrosted chocolate cookies?" he asked.

"Because…" she paused, trying to come up with a rational explanation.

"Aye, because…" he prompted.

"Because it's a custom and the frosting prepares your palate for the chocolate cookies," she finished quickly.

Ian tilted his head and studied her for a moment. "A custom is it?" he asked.

Nodding, she grabbed a cookie from the plate, twisted it open and scraped the frosting from the middle. "A custom," she reiterated, her mouth filled with frosting.

Ian scraped the frosting from the cookie and then took a bite. He chewed carefully, analyzing the flavor sensation of the bare cookie. Finally, he nodded and smiled at Mary. "It does make a difference," he admitted.

She slipped into her chair and shook her head. "Ian, I think I've lost it," she whispered.

He patted her back. "No, darling, you just need a little excitement."

At that moment the phone rang. The two just stared at each other for a moment.

"Well, let's just see if this is an answer to my prayers," she said, picking up the phone. "Mary O'Reilly."

"Hey, Mary, this is Jerry Wiley, at the paper," said the voice on the other end.

Mary smiled. "Yes, Jerry, I remember you."

"Yeah, well, remember when I said there was something that I couldn't remember about the Foley suicide?"

"Yes, I remember, you were going to email me something."

"Yeah, well, maybe you ought to come down here," he said. "'Cause this is something that I want to tell you in person."

"Okay, I'll be down there in fifteen minutes," she replied eagerly.

Then she looked at Ian whose eyebrows were raised and he was shaking his head. "Yeah, and I'll be bringing a friend," Mary said, rolling her eyes at Ian. "He's really good at research, so he'll be helpful. Thanks Jerry."

She hung up the phone and turned to him. "What?" she said, before he had a chance to say anything.

He smiled and leaned back in his chair. "I didna say a word," he said. "But when he gets back tonight, you get to explain this to him."

Mary walked over and turned off the kettle. "Well, as it happens, I have a meeting tonight," she said. "I have to see a person about a ghost."

Ian stood up and grabbed his jacket. "Well, then, you'll be taking your researcher along with you," he said. "Because I'd rather not be the person at home who gets to explain to Bradley where you've gone."

Smiling, Mary offered him her hand. "Deal," she said.

He grinned at her. "Aye, deal."

Chapter Fifteen

Mary had often marveled at the effect beautiful women had on men. Not that she considered herself in that category, but she had seen other, more obviously beautiful women walk into a room and have half of the men nearly fall upon themselves to help her. She hadn't realized, until she and Ian walked into the paper's office that morning that the effect held true when a gorgeous man walked into a room too.

Ian held the door for Mary, and then followed her into the office. Mary watched as the heads of the women in the ad and classified sections lifted from their monitors and watched as he strolled across the room to the reception desk. The receptionist, who earlier that week had been disinterested and sullen, was friendly and, Mary hated to say it, perky, when she saw Ian approach. And Mary heard at least a dozen muffled sighs when he spoke.

"Good morning, darling, we're here to see Jerry Wiley," he said with a smile. "Is he available?"

She sighed. "Are you available?" she wondered aloud, and then realizing what she said, her face turned a dark shade of red.

Ian leaned forward, over the tall reception desk, and took her hand. "Ah, darling, I know you'd just break my heart," he said softly.

Smiling up at him, she stood and just stared at him for a few more moments. Then she shook her head, as if waking from a trance, and took a deep shuddering breath. "I'll just go get him," she said eagerly. "I won't be a minute."

Smiling at her, he nodded. "Thank you."

She half-stumbled, half-jogged across the large room to the entrance of the newsroom, and then disappeared behind the door.

"If you could bottle that, you'd be dangerous," Mary whispered to Ian.

He shrugged, causing all of the muscles under his knit shirt to expand and then contract, and all of the women's heart rates to accelerate. "I canna explain it," he said. "It must be the accent."

She grinned at him. He was really clueless, which was probably part of the charm. "Yeah, that and the shirt," she teased.

"My shirt?" he asked looking down. "What's wrong with my...?"

"Um, Mr. Wiley can see you now," the receptionist announced, as she hurried back across the room.

"Thank you, darling," he said with a smile and then allowed Mary to enter through the security gate first, following her across the room.

"Why the hell did you bring him with you?" Jerry asked as they slipped through the doorway to the newsroom. "Now I'm not going to get any work out of them for a couple of hours."

"What? What did I do?" Ian asked.

"Jerry Wiley, this is Professor Ian MacDougal from the University of Edinburgh," she said.

Jerry's eyebrows raised and he studied Ian again. "He's the guy who wrote that thesis on paranormal phenomenon and electromagnetic residue?"

"Aye, that's me," Ian said.

"Don't you know that you're supposed to be seventy years old with no hair, a pot belly and a pair of glasses?" Jerry asked.

Ian grinned. "Oh, well, I am," he said. "This is naught but my disguise."

Jerry smiled. "Okay, I like this guy," he said to Mary. "Come on back to my office. I think you're going to find this interesting."

They entered his office to find half a dozen newspapers lying on top of his already disorganized desk. Mary picked up the first one and saw it was open to the Obituary page. She scanned it and found the listing for Hope Foley. "This is Hope's obituary," she said. "They don't say suicide."

"Yeah, well, we never say that," he said. "We say 'passed on' or 'left this earth,' things that are less hurtful to the family and friends."

"That makes sense," she replied, picking up the next paper.

She saw that it dated four years later than the first and it too was open to the Obituary page. In the middle of the page was the photo of another young woman, her birthdate was the same year as Hope's, and she too had "passed away."

"What's with this?" Ian asked, reading over Mary's shoulder.

"Another suicide," Jerry said. "From the same class as Hope. And look at the date."

"Isn't that the same date as Hope's death?" Mary asked, astonished.

"Yeah, same day, four years later," Jerry said. "Her name was Mandy, like I told you. Now look at these."

Ian and Mary looked at the other three papers and found obituaries of three other girls from the same class, all who committed suicide.

"Did they make a pact or something?" Ian asked. "They've spaced them exactly four years apart."

"Yeah, and the next one is due this week," Jerry replied. "It will be number five in the series."

"Has anyone linked these deaths together before this?" Mary asked.

Jerry shook his head. "No, four years is a long time to remember dates," he said. "People remember that other girls died, but they don't remember the details."

"So, where can we get a copy of the yearbook from their class?" Ian asked.

Smiling, Jerry nodded with approval. "Yeah, I do like this guy," he repeated as he pulled a yearbook from under the paperwork on his desk. "I pulled one from our research library; just get it back to me when you're done."

"Thank you," Ian said. "I'll bring it back myself."

Pausing for a moment, Jerry shook his head. "No, send O'Reilly. She doesn't make the staff swoon when she walks in the door."

Laughing, Mary extended her hand to Jerry. "Thanks, you've been a great help."

"Oh, no," Jerry said, not shaking her hand. "You're not off that easy. I want first dibs on the story when you solve this case."

"But my client…"

"Yeah, I met your client, and she hired you to be a ghostbuster and get rid of her household problem," he said. "Not solve a mystery like this."

He folded his arms across his chest. "I want the story."

Mary nodded. "Fair enough," she said. "I'll feed you whatever information I can."

Jerry extended his hand. "Agreed?"

Mary shook it. "Agreed."

Chapter Sixteen

Mary and Ian didn't bother moving the car for their next appointment. The Foley Law Offices were only two blocks away from the newspaper. Mary had called before she left the house and had secured an appointment with both the father and daughter.

"And what are you hoping to find?" Ian asked. "Seeing you can't really tell them you're trying to get rid of a ghost."

Mary stopped in the middle of the sidewalk and looked at him. "Don't worry," she said, "I have something brilliant planned."

Ian nodded, and they continued walking up the street. "So, you have absolutely no idea what you're going to say," he stated casually.

"Exactly," Mary replied.

The law offices reflected the status and success of the two lawyers. The ultra-professional administrative assistant politely brought them into the wood-paneled conference room and offered them bottles of sparkling water in crystal glasses with ice while they waited for the Foleys to arrive. Mary sipped delicately and gazed around the room. "I always wanted a room like this," she said. "But I'd have a fireplace and overstuffed leather chairs."

Ian grinned. "And shelves filled with leather books on each wall, with a loft above filled with even more shelves."

Nodding, she leaned toward him. "And one of those really cool library ladders that slide from section to section."

"Aye, it sounds like my library back home," he said.

"Really?" she asked. "Do you really live in a place like that?"

"Well, it's monstrous huge, a bit drafty and a wee bit pretentious, but we like to call it home," he said with a smile.

"How could you ever leave such a place?" she asked.

"Ah, well, that's easy," he said. "To be in your company and be part of your adventures. I can't tell you the fun I've had these past few months."

"Oh, yes, it's been loads of fun," she said, rolling her eyes.

He met her eyes and she was surprised to see how serious he was. "Aye, I've made friends who are like family to me now," he said. "I've been accepted for what I do and who I am. I wouldna have missed this adventure for the world."

She reached over and placed her hand on top of his. "Well, I'm glad you've been part of it too," she said earnestly. "You're family now, Ian."

The turning of the doorknob had Mary pulling her hand away and sitting up in her chair. Mr. Foley was an attractive older man with a full head of salt-

and-pepper hair. His skin was tanned and he looked like he spent a fair amount of time at the gym. His daughter was perfectly coiffed and seemed too sophisticated in her dress and makeup for downtown Freeport. Her suit was tasteful and expensive and her high heels were probably worth more than Mary's entire closet full of clothes.

"Ms. O'Reilly," Mr. Foley said, coming forward to greet her. "I'm Jackson Foley and this is my daughter, Faith. How can we help you?"

"Mr. Foley, Faith, this is Professor Ian MacDougal, my colleague from the University of Edinburgh," she said. "He is here on a fellowship through the University of Chicago."

"Edinburgh?" Mr. Foley repeated, pursing his lips in consideration. "That's an impressive institution, Professor."

"Ian, please," Ian replied. "It's a pleasure to meet both of you."

"No, it's actually our pleasure," Faith said, eyeing Ian directly.

"And why are you here?" Jackson asked Ian.

"Well, I, um," he sent a beseeching look to Mary.

"It's a little awkward for us," Mary interrupted, earning a quick look of gratitude from Ian. "Ian is doing some wonderful research on psychological development, and he has been focusing on teenage suicide. I imagine this is still painful, and I hope you'll forgive us for asking, but we wondered if we could speak with you about Hope's death."

"How did you know about Hope?" Faith asked, her voice just slightly tense.

"Ah, well, we just came from the local paper," Ian said. "Jerry Wiley has been quite helpful."

"And you came to Freeport to study this because?" Jackson asked.

"Well, we needed to find a sister city to the town in Scotland I'm studying," Ian said. "The size and many of the demographics of Freeport are similar to Cambuslang, a small town outside of Glasgow. They too were mainly a rural community until manufacturing came in and changed the footprint of the community. I felt a place similar would give more validity to our findings."

Jackson templed his fingers together and rested his chin on his thumbs, his forefingers pressing against his lips as he pondered Ian's response. Finally, he lowered his hands. "Well, that makes a great deal of sense and we would be happy to help in any way we can," he said. "As a matter of fact, Faith is quite a local advocate of the Stop Bullying movement."

"Good for you," Mary said to Faith. "That's an important message."

Faith nodded. "Yes, if it hadn't been for bullying, my dear sister would still be here," she said, once again her focus on Ian. "I think it's wonderful that you care so much for those who have taken their lives in their youth."

"So, you believe her suicide was instigated by bullying and no other factors?" Ian asked, pulling out a notebook and pen.

"What do you mean by other factors?" Jackson asked.

"Well, some suicides are pacts that teenagers make with one another," he suggested. "Another is a relationship break-up."

"Yes," Mary added. "And some are due to substance abuse, while others are caused by depression."

"No, my sister was bullied," Faith insisted. "There was no way anyone could have taken the abuse that was dished out to my sister."

"Who delivered the abuse?" Mary asked.

"Well, we really don't want to name names," Jackson said. "After all, we still need to live in this community and we don't want to uncover old wounds."

"Well, perhaps you could give us a general idea," Ian suggested. "For example, did she get teased at school? Was there a neighbor who was mean to her? Perhaps a family member."

"Hope loved her family," Faith said. "Everyone in her family."

"That's wonderful," Mary interjected. "But it also shows us that even the love and support of a good family can't prevent tragedy. Who had so much power over Hope that she finally decided she couldn't take it any longer?"

"She wasn't accepted at school," Faith said. "Most of the kids there made fun of her."

"Why?" Ian asked.

Faith shrugged. "Well, she wasn't popular."

"What does it take to be popular?" Ian asked.

She smiled slowly at Ian and leaned her head to the side, her hair brushing against her shoulder. "I think someone like you would know very well what it takes to be popular," she said. "Often popularity is given because of physical appeal, social status, leadership or athletic ability. There is often no rhyme or reason to why some students are chosen and others are not."

Ian turned his whole attention to her. "And those who are popular often make the judgment about who else should be considered popular. Almost a pack or gang mentality."

"Well, yes, that's generally true," she agreed. "The group does tend to decide who joins their ranks."

Encouraging her, Ian smiled and slowly nodded. "And I'd guess that you were one of the popular ones in your high school."

Lowering her eyelids for a moment in false modesty, she then lifted her eyes and smiled back at him. "Well, yes, I guess you could say I was popular."

Ian's smile sobered. "And yet, your sister was not," he said. "Did you not want to offer her the same advantages you had?"

Taken aback, she abruptly sat upright in her chair. "I think you misunderstood the situation," she stated sharply. "I had nothing to do with my sister's death. I supported her. I encouraged her."

"Ah, well, that's good to know," Ian replied.

There was a moment of awkward silence, finally Jackson stood up and turned to Mary. "Well, I'm afraid we have to cut this interview short. But please, if there is anything else we can help you with, don't hesitate to call our offices or send us an email."

Before Mary or Ian could stand and reply, Jackson ushered Faith out the room and the door closed behind them.

"Well, that was interesting," Mary said.

"Aye, I dinna think I charmed her."

Smiling, Mary shrugged her shoulders. "Well, you can't win them all."

Chapter Seventeen

"Guess what I did today?" Clarissa said as she ran from the front door into the kitchen where Mary and Ian were preparing dinner.

"What did you do?" Mary asked.

"I got signed up for school," she replied. "And I'm going to be in Maggie's class."

"School?" Mary asked, looking over Clarissa's head to Bradley. "Well that is a surprise."

Bradley slipped off his coat and hung it on the back of a chair. "Clarissa, why don't you take your backpack up to your room," he suggested. "Then you can tell Mary more about school."

As soon as she dashed up the stairs, Bradley turned to Mary and Ian. "I thought she would be just as safe at school as she would be anywhere else," he said. "And she really needs to get back into a routine."

"You spoke with the principal? She knows about the situation?" Mary asked.

"Yes, I let them know about Gary," he said. "And actually they were more prepared for the situation than I thought they would be. I guess there are quite a few circumstances where children are in danger of being taken by their non-custodial parent."

"It will be nice for her to be back with her friends," Ian agreed. "But Gary is much more dangerous than a non-custodial parent."

Mike appeared in the room next to them. "I'll keep an eye on her too," he said. "Grammar school was always my favorite anyway."

Mary turned to him. "And what will you do when Clarissa or Maggie ask you a question in front of the teacher?" she asked.

"Pass them a note?" Mike teased and then he shook his head. "No, I'll be in stealth mode when I'm at the school. The girls don't need to know I'm there unless there's trouble. Most guardian angels and ghosts, for that matter, stay in stealth most of the time anyway."

Mary sat down on one of chairs at the kitchen table and exhaled slowly. "I know this is the right thing," she said. "But…"

"You're scared to death," Bradley added.

"Yes, I am," she replied.

"I believe that's part and parcel of being a parent," Ian said.

Bradley walked over to Mary and knelt down beside her. He took her hand in his. "If you are uncomfortable with this, I'll pull her out of school," he said.

Shaking her head, she wrapped both of her hands around his. "No. No, you're right. She needs her life to get back to normal more than anything else. And Mike will be there," she said. "She's better watched over than any of the children there."

Mike grinned. "You'd be surprised to learn how many guardian angels go to school each day."

The conversation was halted when they heard the sound of little feet coming back down the stairs. "And guess what?" Clarissa was asking even before she reached the bottom steps.

"What?" Mary called.

"I already have homework."

"That's amazing," Mary replied. "What do you get to do?"

"I get to read a book and answer some questions," she said. "Can I read it to you?"

Mary's heart warmed and she nodded. "I would love to have you read," she said.

She stood up and led Clarissa to the couch. "Shall we read here?" she asked.

"Sure," Clarissa responded, climbing up next to her.

With Mary's arm around her, Clarissa nestled closer and began to read while Bradley helped Ian make the rest of the dinner. Halfway through the book, Clarissa stopped and looked up at Mary. "Can the bad man get me at school?" she whispered, watching to be sure Bradley didn't hear her.

Mary looked down at her and shook her head. "Your daddy, Bradley, talked to the principal at your school about the bad man, so they are going to be watching to make sure you're safe. And Mike is going to be there to protect you. And, because you are very smart and very aware, you are going to watch and be careful until we find him, right?"

She nodded. "Right. I'm not going to go near any strangers."

"Exactly," Mary said. "And your daddy and I will keep working on catching him, so you won't have any worries."

Clarissa looked up at Mary for a moment, a questioning look on her face. "If Bradley is my daddy and he's going to marry you, will you be my mommy?"

Mary's heart melted as she looked down on the dear little face. "I'd really like to be your mommy," she said. "I have always wanted to have a little girl."

"Is it okay for a kid to have three mommies?" she asked.

Smiling down at her, Mary nodded. "Oh, sure, that just gives you more people who love you."

"Can I come to your wedding?"

"Oh, yes, sweetheart," she replied. "And I would love to have you be my flower girl."

"Would I have to walk up the aisle?"

Mary nodded. "Yes, you would. We'd get you a special dress and you would sprinkle flower petals on the ground. Does that sound like fun?"

"Could Maggie do it too?" she asked. "So there could be two of us?"

Mary placed a kiss on Clarissa's forehead. "Oh, that would be perfect," she said. "Two beautiful flower girls. I love that idea."

Clarissa smiled up at her. "Me too."

"Now, we need to finish the rest of this book," Mary reminded her. "So we can eat dinner."

Clarissa met Mary's eyes one more time. "Thanks for being my new mommy," she said.

Mary placed another kiss on the top of her head. "It is my pleasure."

Chapter Eighteen

"So, the owner didna want to meet us here?" Ian asked later that night, as they pulled the car around the circular drive and parked in front of the door.

"Nope, she just handed me the keys and told me to return them to her once the ghost was gone," Mary replied.

"Well, I suppose we can cross her off the list as possible recruits for a paranormal activities society," Ian teased.

"Yes, I think that's a safe bet," Mary laughed as she got out of the car.

They walked up the steps to the front door. "It doesn't look like your typical haunted house," Ian said, gazing around at the lavish upscale estate.

"That's the funny thing about haunted houses," Mary replied as she stuck the key into the lock. "You just can never tell when one will pop up."

Mary pushed the door open and then turned and helped Ian carry his equipment into the foyer. "I've never used electronic equipment before," she said. "Do you think I ought to add it to my process?"

"Well, darling, it just depends on what you want to do," he said, as they carried several large cases of equipment upstairs to the second floor. "If you're trying to record things for scientific measurement and annals, then you need all this crap. But if you're just trying to help a soul move from one realm to the other, you just need your natural ability."

Mary opened the case that held the video camera and set it up on a tripod, facing the middle of the room. "You won't see what I see on the video, will you?" she asked.

Ian shook his head. "No, that's highly unlikely to get such a clear picture," he said. "But we'll probably get some orbs, we may get a shadow and the camera has a sensitive recording device for picking up EVPs."

"EVPs?"

"Electronic Voice Phenomena," he replied. "There's a belief that spirits try to communicate with us and we can pick up their words through enhanced electronic recording equipment."

"Does it work?"

As Ian attached the cables to other equipment and set it up around the circumference of the room, he responded to her question, "Well, generally the sound is so faint or garbled it's anyone's best guess what the ghost was communicating. And often, if the investigators have clues beforehand, they might be biased toward thinking it was something relating to the clues."

"So why are we doing it?" Mary asked, pulling a small Digital EMF Meter from another case.

"Well, in this case, where you can actually view the entity, it might be interesting background to see if we can pick anything up and then apply this case toward other, less visual, paranormal investigations."

"Okay, well, you can stand over here with this and see if you can actually pick up any electromagnetic readings when she shows up," Mary said. "And I'll be over here, to see if she'll actually speak with me."

They moved into place and waited. But they didn't have to wait very long. The atmosphere in the room began to change; Mary actually felt a chill as the temperature began to drop and she rubbed her hands over her arms.

Ian looked down at his EMF Meter and saw the slender arm raise as it registered the phenomenon taking place in the room.

Mary didn't need Ian's machine to feel the electricity in the air. It was as if someone had opened a portal from another place and the room was being filled with a kind of ectoplasmic fog. She tensed; the hairs on the back of her neck standing on end as she held her breath.

The ghost appeared in the corner of the room, translucent and glowing. Her body was slightly turned, her arms were outstretched, as if she were re-enacting pulling something across the room. A muffled sound, like something being dragged across the carpeted floor, seemed to echo from all corners of the room.

Dressed in pajamas, her long hair was caught back in a ponytail, and her feet were bare. She stopped in the middle of the room, underneath the ceiling fan and slowly turned, gazing around the room. Her macabre smile seemed eager as she ran to the closet door and tied something tightly around the knob. She hurried back to the center of the room and climbed up on the invisible object that she had pulled to the spot.

Standing mid-air, she continued her preparations as she tossed something over the fan. Although she couldn't see the object, Mary knew the ghost was throwing a cord over the fan.

Tugging on the end of the invisible cord, the ghost smiled again and turned toward the bedroom door. No more than a minute passed before the door slowly opened. Ian, who'd been standing next to it, jumped out of the way and sent Mary a look of startled surprise. She replied with a quick nod and then turned her attention back to see the ghost's reaction.

The ghost's smile widened. She looked down at the door and her mouth was moving, although neither Mary nor Ian could hear what she was saying. Because her face was translucent and was shifting in the low light of the room, Mary had a hard time reading her facial expressions, but she didn't seem upset or startled. It was as if she had been expecting her visitor.

With a shake of her head and a laugh, the ghost seemed to be placing the cord over her head. She held her hand out to the side, as if she held the end of a noose with it. Then she pulled it sharply to the side for a moment and bent her head, mimicking someone who'd been hanged. A moment later, she clapped her hands together and laughed at her visitor.

Moving around the elevated platform with confidence, she pointed and laughed at her visitor. Suddenly the bedroom door slammed shut with great force.

Both Mary and Ian jumped at the sound, and then turned quickly because the ceiling fan started to turn on its own. The ghost's smile quickly faded as she looked up at the fan. She screamed silently toward the door, and began to frantically pull at the cord around her neck. She was slowly lifted upward as if the cord was being wrapped around the rotating fan. She struggled and they both heard a thump on the carpet in front of them, as if the platform had tipped over.

Desperately, the girl clawed at the cord, gasping and crying as she struggled. She tossed and fought for several minutes, until finally her arms fell limply to her sides, her head rolled to her shoulder and she hung, lifelessly, slowly rotating in the middle of the room.

Turning from the macabre vision, Mary looked at Ian. He was leaning back against the wall, his face ashen and his eyes still locked on the ghost.

"Ian," she whispered.

He turned to her and it seemed as if he didn't know her, his face reflecting hopelessness and sorrow. He seemed vulnerable and lost.

She crossed the room and placed her hand on his arm. "Ian, are you okay?"

Shaking his head quickly, he looked over at Mary and took a deep, shaky breath. "I'm sorry," he said, trying to mask his emotions with a smile. "This one hit closer to home than usual."

"What happened?" she asked.

He shook his head. "I'll tell you another time," he said softly, "and I thank you for your concern. But I think we need to get back to our ghost."

They both looked up at the ghost again. Her face was slightly bloated and turning purple. Her lips were swollen and her head was lying sideways. Suddenly her eyes burst open and she stared directly at them. A moment later, she was gone.

The atmosphere in the room abruptly changed back to normal and both Mary and Ian inhaled deeply.

"I dinna think what we just saw here was a suicide," he said softly, his heart still racing from the experience.

Shaking her head, Mary slowly moved away from Ian and toward the center of the room, staring at the ceiling fan. "Someone else knew the truth," she said slowly, wiping the residual tears from her face. "Someone else left the room just before Hope died. Why didn't they tell the truth?"

"Aye, and now there's your mystery."

Chapter Nineteen

After packing up Ian's electronic gear, the ride back to the house was completed with minimal conversation as both Mary and Ian contemplated what they had just witnessed.

"Do you ever get used to it?" Ian asked quietly as he stared out the window into the night sky.

Shaking her head, Mary took a deep breath before answering. "No, you never do," she replied. "And if you start to, you need to step away because you are losing your humanity."

They drove in silence for a few more minutes. "Were you able to hear anything she was saying?" Ian asked.

"I thought I would hear a whisper, but nothing intelligible," Mary said, as she turned the car onto her street, she glanced over to him. "And I have to admit I'm grateful that I didn't have to hear her struggle for her life. It was bad enough to watch it."

"Aye, you're right," Ian said. "And it was frustrating to know it happened twenty years ago and there isn't a damned thing you can do about it now."

She pulled into the driveway and turned to him. "Thank you for coming with me. I'm really glad I wasn't alone."

"No one should have been alone to witness that," he said with a nod.

"And yet she was," Mary replied, staring out the front of the car, "all alone when she died."

"Well, we don't know that," Ian said. "All we know is that a door slammed. The visitor could have still been in the room, watching her suffer."

Startled, Mary turned to him. "Do you really think…?"

"Well, hopefully we caught a little more with the equipment," he said. "But until we know for sure, we have to be open to any possibility."

Mary rubbed her arms with her hands. "Picturing someone watching her die and not trying to help makes her death seem even worse."

The house was quiet when they opened the door. Their arms were filled with Ian's equipment. "I wonder where Bradley is," Mary whispered as they moved to the kitchen table.

"Probably putting the wee bairn to bed," Ian said, "and enjoying every minute of it."

Smiling, she nodded her agreement. "He really is enjoying being a father," she agreed.

A few minutes later, as they were setting up the equipment, Bradley came down the stairs. "So, how did it go?" he asked.

"Is Clarissa in bed?" Mary asked.

He nodded. "Yes, she's sound asleep. I just left her."

"Then come over here," she invited. "We need to look this over right away, while the experience is still fresh in our minds."

Ian nodded, placed his case next to the table and slipped off his coat. "I'll run upstairs and get my laptop," he said. "Then we'll see what we captured."

"Captured?" Bradley asked Mary as Ian headed up the stairs.

"Ian brought his electronic equipment with him this time," she said. "We're hoping it picked up some things we couldn't."

Ian came back down and attached the equipment to a control box that was plugged into a USB port on the side of his laptop. He pressed a few buttons and the girl's bedroom came into view. The camera scanned the entire room and then stayed focused on the middle of the room. There was a box on the bottom of the screen with a series of numbers in separate boxes.

"What's that?" Bradley asked.

"The first box is the reading from the Digital EMF recorder," Ian said. "You'll see that as we set up the equipment, the numbers are pretty low, from 0mg to 1.5mg. If it is able to read the ghost Mary saw, you'll see readings that can go as high as 8mg."

"And this number," Bradley asked, pointing to the next box.

"That's the digital thermometer reading," he replied.

"I know, cold spots, right," Bradley said.

"Aye, but there can also be hot spots at times," Ian said. "Any reading plus or minus ten is a sign of paranormal activity."

"Okay, the third set?"

"That's the infrared meter," Ian explained. "The video camera works with infrared lighting because it's been theorized that paranormal entities are more visible in infrared. This meter sends out a beam of infrared light and relays the temperature of the surface."

"So, does this stuff really work?" Bradley asked, watching the screen over Ian's shoulder.

"Well, we're about to find out," Ian said. "This is the first time I've tested it when I know there's an entity in the room."

The video initially focused on Mary. Showing her standing across the room from the lens. The conversation she and Ian shared had ended and she was just waiting for something to happen. Then the recording showed her rubbing her hands over her arms as the temperature had begun to drop in the room.

"And here we go," Ian whispered, his attention on the information.

They watched as the entire scene transpired; although the camera only picked up sparks of electromagnetic activity, it did not record the ghost the way both Mary and Ian saw her. The readings continued to monitor the activity in the room. Ian turned the volume up on the audio equipment, and even though he was able to filter out most of the unwanted noise, most of the information was unintelligible.

"Wait, play that part again," Mary said, as they got toward the end of the tape.

Ian reversed the feed and played it again. They all heard what sounded like a girl's voice.

"Can you slow it down?" Bradley asked, leaning closer.

Ian reversed the feed and slowed the playback. They all stood silently, staring at the screen and concentrating on the sounds until they all clearly heard the young woman whisper as her life was nearly over, "No hope."

Chapter Twenty

The smells of breakfast greeted Clarissa as she stood at the top of the stairs. She stopped and looked at Mike, her face filled with concern. "Do they really love me?" she asked.

He squatted down next to her, so he could look into her eyes. "Yes, they really do," he said. "They loved you before they even met you, because of who you were. Now they love you even more because of who you are."

She nodded, contemplating his answer for a moment. "Is it bad...I mean, I love my mommy, Becca, and my daddy, Henry...but is it bad that I love Bradley and Mary too?"

"No, sweetheart," Mike reassured her. "Love isn't like a pie. There isn't just so much to go around and then you don't have any more. Love keeps growing and expanding. Your little heart can love as many people as you want."

The worry slipped from her face and she smiled at him. "Thank you for bringing me here," she said. "I really do love it."

"You're welcome," he replied. "Besides, this is where you belong."

She started to go down the steps when suddenly she stopped and turned to him. "Oh, I almost forgot," she said. "I love you too Mike."

He stood and watched her skip down the steps to the kitchen.

"Good morning to you," Ian said, as he met Mike at the top of the staircase.

"Morning," Mike said, his voice slightly hoarse. "I learned something already today."

"Aye, and what would that be?" Ian asked.

"Angels can cry," Mike said, wiping a tear from his cheek and studying it with curiosity.

Ian nodded. "I admit to overhearing the conversation you had with Clarissa, and it's no small wonder that she loves you."

Mike couldn't explain the overwhelming emotion he felt from hearing Ian's words. *What? Did becoming an angel turn a guy into a wimp?*

"Knock it off, Scotty," he finally said. "You're not going to make me cry too."

Laughing, Ian nodded and started down the steps. "Well, then, I'm off to eat waffles."

Mike followed. "Oh, yeah, eating food, rub it in."

He followed Ian down the stairs and they both paused at the doorway of the kitchen with an unspoken agreement as they watched Mary and Bradley helping Clarissa at the table. Bradley was leaning over cutting waffles into bite-sized pieces and Mary was pouring more milk into a small glass. Clarissa already had a mouth full of food and she was eagerly telling both of them a story.

"Looks good, doesn't it?" Mike whispered to Ian.

"Aye, they're already a family," he replied softly.

They entered the kitchen and Mary looked up and smiled. "Good morning," she said. "There are waffles warming in the oven and bacon on the plate next to the stove."

Ian approached the table and smiled. "'Tis a braw sight to see, this family of yours."

He leaned over Mary's chair and kissed her lightly on the cheek, then turned and kissed Clarissa too. He stood up and moved toward Bradley.

"You try kissing me and there's going to be problems," Bradley said, his voice stern but his smile belying his words.

"I don't think I could stomach that before breakfast," Ian replied, moving over to the kitchen counter to get a plate from the cabinet. "But your lassies were just too hard to resist."

Bradley got up from the table and walked over to Ian, snatching a piece of bacon from the plate. "Mary, do you need anything?" he asked.

She smiled at him, but shook her head. "No, I'm good, thanks."

"You're a lucky man, Bradley Alden," Ian said softly.

Bradley glanced at Mary and Clarissa and then turned to Ian. "Luckier than I ever thought possible," he replied, keeping his voice low. "Can you keep an eye on Mary today? Without her knowing you're doing it?"

Ian grinned. "Oh, aye, I'm a fairly crafty fellow, she'll never know."

Bradley bit into the bacon. "Thanks. Mike will be with Clarissa and I'll be checking on her throughout the day. But Mary…"

"She's a mind of her own," Ian finished. "We'll be working on the new case together, so you've no need to worry."

"Until they've caught that bastard and put him some place safe and secure, I'm going to worry," he replied.

"Don't you think he's long gone by now? He had a passport and money, why would he stay here?"

Leaning against the counter, Bradley turned so his back was to Mary. "That would be the actions of a sane man," he said quietly. "Gary Copper is unstable, to say the least. Whatever is driving him now, whatever is motivating him, will influence his actions. Common sense or even self-preservation may not be his driving force."

Ian glanced at Mary over Bradley's shoulder; she was busy with Mike and Clarissa. He turned back to Bradley. "He'd be willing to die in order to exact revenge?" he asked quietly, his jaw clenched in anger. "I've studied terrorism and fanaticism; experts say it's virtually impossible to stop someone who is prepared to die for his cause."

Bradley nodded slowly.

"And you've shared this with her?" Ian asked.

Bradley glanced back to make sure Mary was still occupied. "She understands he's a threat," he

111

said. "But because of the trauma she's already experienced, I don't think she wants to give him that much power. She is treating him like any other escaped convict."

"Does that make her more vulnerable?"

"Not if we're watching out for her too."

Ian picked up a piece of bacon and snapped it in half. "Aye, I'll be watching," he said.

"Thank you."

"No need to thank me," he replied. "She has a piece of my heart as well. None of us want anything to happen to our Mary."

Chapter Twenty-one

Bradley, Clarissa and Mike left a few minutes later in a flurry of backpacks, lunch boxes, hugs and kisses. Mary dropped onto the couch, her eyes closed and her head resting against the overstuffed cushions. "This is exhausting," she said. "How do parents do this every morning?"

Laughing, Ian sat on the arm of the couch and looked down at her. "Well, I think they must develop a system," he said. "And, of course, most parents don't cook a three-course meal for breakfast."

Mary opened her eyes and glared at him. "I wanted her to have a nourishing breakfast," she replied. "You know, breakfast is the most important meal of the day."

She closed her eyes again, but then they popped back open. "You don't think I made too much, do you?" she asked, horrified. "You don't think I'm encouraging childhood obesity?"

Shaking his head, Ian said, "She was happy, she was fed, she was warm..." He paused. "And any other comfort a child might need on her first day of school. You did fine, Mary. You're a good mom."

The reality of the situation finally hit home. "Ian, I'm a mom," she whispered, her voice thick with emotion. "I mean, you know, not really..."

He placed his hand over hers. "Aye, really, you're a mom," he repeated. "And you're doing a fine job of it."

She couldn't find her voice for several moments. "Thank you, Ian," she finally whispered.

"I did naught but tell the truth," he replied. "So, now, what's in the plan for today?"

Taking a deep breath, she sat up and turned to him again. "Oh, you mean besides having you watch over me like a hawk?"

He grinned. "Aye, besides that."

"I think we ought to talk to Hope's mother," Mary said. "I got a feeling that Faith and her father weren't telling us everything they knew about that night."

"Aye, and if there was a person who knew about the hanging and didn't do anything, they could be an accessory to murder," he said. "But how do we find out which home she's staying in?"

Mary walked over to her computer and did a search on nursing homes in the Freeport area. She looked through the list, noting the ones that were more upscale than the others. " I think we should start with this one first," she said, pointing to the facility that was situated next to Krape Park.

"Why?" Ian asked.

"Because I have a contact there," Mary said, "and because it's been around the longest."

She dialed the number. "Hello, may I speak with Jennika Nikole please?" she asked.

"This is Jennika," the woman on the other end replied.

"Hello, Jennika, I met you a few months ago when I was in visiting Ross Gormley. My name is Mary O'Reilly," she said.

"Oh, yes, Miss O'Reilly, I remember you," Jennika replied. "How can I help you?"

"I'm supposed to be interviewing a woman today, regarding a research investigation I'm working on," she said. "But I'm embarrassed to admit, I didn't write down which nursing home she lived in. I know that she's quite well-to-do and her family wanted her to be very well cared for, so I just assumed she was at your facility."

"Well, thank you, Miss O'Reilly," Jennika replied, pleasure evident in her voice. "I can check and see if she's one of our residents. What's her name?"

"Gloria," Mary answered. "Gloria Foley."

"Oh, yes, I don't even need to look it up," she said. "Mrs. Foley is one of our residents."

Mary looked over at Ian and gave him a thumbs-up signal. "That's wonderful," Mary replied. "Do you know…is she available this morning? I'd love to be able to speak with her today."

"Yes," Jennika said. "She's already had breakfast and she's just resting in the sunroom. I'm sure she would love to speak with you, she rarely has visitors."

Mary smiled at Ian and shook her head. "Well, excellent, I will be there in about twenty minutes," she replied. "And I'll be bringing a colleague of mine, a professor from the University of Edinburgh who is conducting the study."

"I'm sure that will be fine, Miss O'Reilly," Jennika said. "We'll see you then."

Mary hung up the phone and turned to Ian who was still dressed in sweatpants and a t-shirt. "Can you get ready and look professorly in fifteen minutes?"

"I can," he said, jumping up from the couch.

"Oh, can you bring your recording device?" Mary asked.

"I can, yes," he replied. "But why?"

"Just in case Gloria's daughter comes to see her mother during our visit."

Chapter Twenty-two

Gloria Foley was still a very attractive woman, although her hair was now liberally sprinkled with silver threads and the corners of her eyes showed the lines of age. She was dressed in a silk caftan in bright jeweled colors and rings of the same hues sparkled on her fingers. Mary watched her eyes as they approached and was relieved to see openness and welcome in them.

"Hello, Mrs. Foley," Mary said when they reached the elegant rattan chair she was seated in. "My name is Mary O'Reilly and this is my colleague, Professor Ian MacDougal from the University of Edinburgh."

"Oh, from Scotland?" she asked, motioning for them to take seats near her. "How very interesting."

"Ach, well, not so verra interesting," Ian said, thickening his accent a little for effect. "But I canna deny it holds a special place in me heart."

"I'm sure it would," Gloria responded. "I visited there once and I fell in love with it."

"Did you?" he asked. "And when was that?"

"Oh, it was the year before..." She stopped and her face changed, a veil of sadness covering it. "It was a while ago."

"Mrs. Foley, we'd like to ask you some questions that might bring back some sad memories," Mary said. "Are you willing to speak with us?"

"Sad memories?" Gloria asked. "Why do you need to ask me questions like that?"

Ian scooted his chair a little closer to hers and took her hand in his. "I'm doing research about adolescents and suicides," he said. "And I'm hoping you will speak to us to help other children."

Gloria looked down at her hand clasped in his and then slowly looked up and met his eyes. "She had no reason to kill herself," she whispered. "Everyone loved her. I don't understand…"

"I read the police report," Mary said. "You were the one who found your daughter."

Gloria turned to Mary and nodded. "I was just checking on her, like I did every night," she said. "To be sure she was safe…"

Her voice shook and she took a deep breath. "I tried to help her…tried to lift her up…but I wasn't strong enough," she explained. "If only I'd been stronger…"

"No, that wouldna helped," Ian said. "She was gone before you found her."

She looked at Ian. "Are you sure?" she asked. "How can you know?"

"I know," he assured her. "And I'm sure."

She slipped her hand out from his clasp and searched in the pockets of her caftan for a handkerchief. Drawing it out and turning away from them and toward the window, she dabbed away the moisture from around her eyes. "They…the authorities…told me that too. I just always thought…"

"Aye, if there was only something I had done or something I had said," Ian added softly.

She looked at him, grateful for his understanding. "Yes. Yes, what could I have done to prevent it?" she said.

"And that's why we're here today, speaking with you," Ian replied. "To try and find out some of those answers."

"Will your study help find out what happened to my daughter?" she asked.

"That's one of our goals," Mary answered honestly. "We want to find out the truth and use that to help prevent other deaths."

Gloria took a deep breath, placed her folded hands on her lap and faced them. "Ask me what you will," she said. "I get a little confused sometimes, but I will try my best."

"That's all we're asking for, darling," Ian said.

"We'll take it slow," Mary added.

"Now, tell us about the day it happened," Ian said.

"Well, I remember that Hope had been quite dramatic that day. She was upset about Faith and her boyfriend. She actually accused Faith of maliciously trying to steal her boyfriends. I explained to her that Faith couldn't help being popular."

119

"Was there any boy in particular involved with Hope at the time?" Mary asked.

"Oh, yes," Gloria paused, searching her memory. "He was a strange young man; not at all someone Faith would be interested in. It was obviously a one-sided attraction. He liked computer games and role-playing. Always talking about swords and knives."

She shuddered. "I always wondered if he had talked her into killing herself. He seemed to be the type that would find glory in death."

"Did you mention that to the police?" Mary asked.

Shaking her head, Gloria said, "Oh, no, her death was obviously a suicide. Why would I implicate someone else?"

"Do you remember his name?" Ian asked.

"It was…something…foreign sounding," she said slowly, trying to remember. "Nickolas. That was it, Nickolas."

"Do you recall his last name?" Mary asked.

She shook her head and appeared to be a little confused for a moment. "No, just Nickolas. It's been such a long time and after she died, well, I lost track of a lot of things."

"How did Faith react to her sister's death?" Mary asked.

Turning away from both of them, she stared out the window for a few minutes. She dabbed the handkerchief against the corners of her eyes and finally took a deep trembling breath. "Faith died that

120

day," Gloria said, and then she shook her head. "It was so awful. So we had to send her away."

She looked back at them, her eyes filled with remorse. "We had to do it," she tried to explain. "No one would believe that Faith…"

Pausing for a moment, she seemed to be concentrating on something in the back of her mind. "No one will believe us," she said softly, not seeming to be aware of Mary and Ian any longer. "They will think she murdered her sister. We have to send her away where she will be safe."

She looked up at them. "I didn't want her to go," she confessed. "He did, my husband, the lawyer. He said people would talk. They would always blame her. There was no reason she would have killed herself. She had so much to live for."

"He thought people would blame Faith?" Mary asked. "So he sent her away?"

Gloria turned to Mary and shook her head. "He sent her away and she came back a different person," she said, and then her eyes filled with tears. "I lost both of my daughters that day."

Chapter Twenty-three

Clarissa and Maggie skipped hand in hand from the school into the playground for recess. A few other girls joined them, girls that remembered Clarissa from her early days in Freeport. "We're the 'doption girls again," Maggie said. "And we're always going to be best friends."

Clarissa thought about it for a moment. "But I'm not 'dopted anymore," she said. "Daddy Bradley is my real daddy."

Maggie stopped skipping and let go of Clarissa's hand. Ever since she saw Clarissa with Mike, she had felt a little left out. Mike had been her friend. He had watched over her when she stayed with Mary. And now Mary was going to be Clarissa's mommy. She probably wouldn't have time to do things together, like they used to do. It wasn't fair. Clarissa was ruining everything.

"No he's not," Maggie said angrily. "He's not your real dad."

"Yes he is," Clarissa said. "He told me."

Maggie shook her head. "No. No, you're still just 'dopted," she said. "Bradley and Mary are just being nice 'cause they feel sorry for you and don't have their own kids."

Clarissa's heart was pounding and she was getting frightened. *Could Maggie be telling the truth? Were the others just lying?*

She looked around for Mike and saw him standing next to the door. *He would know, he would tell her the truth. Angels couldn't lie.*

Maggie turned to see where Clarissa was looking. She was a little ashamed of her behavior, and she didn't want Mike to know she'd been bad. "Mike can't say anything," Maggie said. "They all lied to you because they want you to feel better. So, it's a white lie and even angels can tell white lies."

Clarissa turned back to Maggie, her eyes filled with tears and her lips trembling. "Bradley's really not my daddy?" she asked.

Maggie, feeling a pit growing in her stomach, forced herself to shake her head. "No, you're still just a 'doption girl, just like me."

"But you have a family," Clarissa whispered. "And they love you and will keep you forever."

Turning away from Maggie, she wiped her face with her mittened hands. "I still don't have anybody."

She ran away from Maggie to the far end of the playground, crying as she ran.

Tears of remorse pooled in Maggie's eyes. She knew she had been purposefully mean and she thought she wanted to hurt Clarissa. But hurting Clarissa hadn't made her feel better, it actually had made her feel much worse. She had to tell someone what she'd done.

She looked over and saw Mike watching her. She hated that Mike would be disappointed in her, but she knew she had to confess.

Hurrying over to him, she wiped the tears from her eyes. "Mike, I just did something very bad," she said.

Mike glanced over and saw that Clarissa was still within the gated security of the playground and turned his attention to Maggie. He squatted down in front of her and met her eyes. "Okay, kid, spill it," he said. "What did you do?"

Clarissa didn't know what to do. *Had they all really lied? If Bradley isn't my daddy, then who is? Why did my mommy give me up? Why did my daddy let her? Doesn't anyone really love me?*

She wandered close to the wrought-iron gate at the edge of the schoolyard.

"What's wrong sweetheart?"

Clarissa looked up to see a man standing on the other side of the fence. She backed up two steps.

"Hey, I'm sorry," he said. "I didn't mean to startle you. You just looked so sad."

"I am sad," she said.

"Well, a pretty little girl like you shouldn't be sad," he said. "I'm sure you have a lot to be happy about."

She shook her head. "No, I don't. My mommy's dead and my daddy's dead. And no one loves me."

"Well, if I had a little girl like you, I'd love her," the man said. "I would take her to wonderful places all around the world and buy her all kinds of wonderful things."

Wiping her eyes again, she studied him for a moment. "You would?"

He nodded. "Yes, I would, Clarissa."

"How do you know my name?" she asked, suddenly fearful.

"Because, sweetheart, I'm your real daddy," he said.

She froze, her heart pounding in her chest. "You're the bad man," she whispered through stiff lips.

He shook his head sadly. "No, sweetheart, I'm the good man," he replied. "I'm just misunderstood."

He took an envelope out of his coat pocket and tossed it to her. "Now you take this and give it to Bradley," he said. "Don't give it to anyone else. Promise?"

She nodded slowly and picked up the envelope and put it in her pocket.

"Good girl," he said with a smile. "Now go back to school before someone misses you. I'll come back and see you another time."

Clarissa turned and ran back toward the school. She was almost to the door when she turned and looked back to the fence. The man was gone.

Mike appeared next to her and she jumped. "Hey, are you okay?" he asked.

She nodded, but didn't meet his eyes. "I have to get back in before I'm late," she said, and turned from him and ran back into the school.

Chapter Twenty-four

Mary unlocked the door to her office and Ian followed her into the building. "Thanks for the detour, this won't take more than a few minutes," she said, as she headed toward her desk.

Ian slipped off his jacket and tossed it onto the back of the chair in front of her desk. "While you're checking your phone messages, I'll visit your facilities," he said, walking over to the bathroom and closing the door.

Mary pressed the button next to the flashing red light and heard, "You have two new messages."

She picked up a notepad and pen and waited for the first message.

"Hello, Mary. Mary O'Reilly? This is Faye Vyas. I was just wondering if you had any updates for me. Did you get a chance to go back to the house last night? Were you able to get rid of whatever it is that's haunting us? Please get back to me."

Mary reached over and pressed the delete button and then the second message started and the pen and pad slipped out of her hands.

"Hello Mary. Have you missed me? I've been thinking about you. Thinking about your soft skin and the way it felt beneath my hands. I know you liked it, Mary. I know you would have been writhing with pleasure beneath me if only we hadn't been

interrupted. And Mary, next time I'll make sure we have plenty of uninterrupted time together…"

Ian clicked off the machine and very nearly picked it up and threw it against the wall. When he had walked out of the bathroom and saw Mary, her fist pressed against her stomach, her face white with fear, and then had heard Gary's voice, anger had been his first response. By the time he'd reached her desk, he realized they would need the recording as evidence and so he only shut it off.

He took hold of Mary's arms and turned her toward him. "Mary, are you…?"

She looked up in shock, and then pushed past him and ran into the bathroom. He heard her emptying the contents of her stomach into the toilet and when she was done, followed her into the bathroom. Pulling the hand towel from the rack, he dampened it with cold water, knelt down next to Mary and handed it to her. "Here, darling, wipe your face," he murmured. "That a girl."

She mopped her face roughly and sat back against the wall. "I can't believe I let him get to me," she said angrily.

He got up and walked out of the room. Mary heard her small refrigerator open and then heard the metallic hiss of a pop can being opened. She smiled with gratitude when Ian handed her a Diet Pepsi and then sat down next to her. "Thanks," she said between sips.

"How are you feeling?" he asked.

"Like an idiot," she replied, her words bitten off in anger.

"Well, then, it's a good thing."

"What's a good thing?" she asked, turning to him, the Diet Pepsi can frozen halfway to her mouth.

"It's a good thing I didn't take you out to lunch before we came to your office," he replied with a smile. "It would have been such a waste."

A slight smile flitted across her lips. "Shut up," she said.

Grinning, he nodded. "Aye, and there's the Mary we all know and love."

"Ian, I let him get to me again," she said. "I let him win."

"He caught you unaware, darling, it was a sneak attack," he said. "He'll not get that chance again."

She shook her head. "No, he won't."

"And he made a major mistake."

"What? What mistake?" she asked.

"You're not just cautious or even afraid anymore, you're angry," he said. "And an angry Mary O'Reilly is very dangerous."

Smiling broadly, she took a gulp of Diet Pepsi, jumped up and offered Ian a hand. A little confused, he took her hand and stood. "What's this?" he asked.

"I just realized that I'm not only angry, I'm starving, and you offered to pay for lunch."

"Sit down or drive-through?" he asked.

She thought about it for a moment. "Drive through," she decided. "That way we can work on both of these cases. Gary Copper won't know what hit him."

"And when we call Bradley..." he began, as they walked toward the front door.

"No," she interrupted.

"What?"

"No, we don't need to call Bradley," she insisted. "Gary's call could have been made from Canada, for all we know. Bradley's got enough on his mind right now. We don't need to worry him."

Ian stopped walking, folded his arms over his chest and leaned against the wall. "Mary, do you think he's not always worrying about you and Clarissa?"

Sighing, she shook her head. "No, I know he's worried. But there's nothing he can do about a phone message, is there?"

Thinking it over for a minute, Ian realized she was right. "But he needs to know," he insisted.

Walking back over to her desk, she unplugged the answering machine. Then she picked up the phone, pressed a few buttons and put the receiver back on the cradle. "Okay, I forwarded my calls to the house and I have the answering machine for evidence," she said. "I'll give it to him tonight."

Ian walked over and took the machine from her, tucking it under his arm. "Well done, Mary. And now, what do we want for lunch?"

"Oh, anything sounds good to me," she replied.

"How about Chinese?" he asked.

"Anything but that," she replied.

"Okay, how about Mexican?"

"I don't know if I want Mexican..."

"Mary, why don't you decide? It will make my life so much easier."

Chapter Twenty-five

Ian carried in the bucket of fried chicken and the side items and Mary carried in their soft drinks. She held both drinks in one arm as she struggled with the door lock and finally got it open. Ian brought the bags directly to the kitchen and immediately opened the small box of hot wings. "I'll never get enough of these," he said, munching on a wing. "Although I'm a bit surprised they didn't offer haggis as a side dish."

Mary put the drinks on the counter and pulled a couple of paper plates from the cabinet. "You're kidding me, right?" she asked, with a skeptical look at Ian. "They don't offer haggis as a side dish at any KFC, not even the ones in Scotland."

"Oh, aye, they do," he teased. "It's right up there on the sign next to the mashed potatoes and the colcannon."

"Colcannon?"

"You mean to tell me you don't have colcannon here either?" he said, his smile giving way to a grin.

"You're a terrible liar, Ian MacDougal," Mary said with a laugh as she scooped out a serving of the mashed potatoes and coleslaw. "And what, may I ask, is in colcannon?"

"It's fair delicious, Mary. It's made from boiled cabbage, carrots, turnips and potatoes, with some butter thrown in for good measure."

"It sounds a bit like my mother's Irish stew without the meat," she replied, taking a bite of her food. "And I don't think she uses boiled cabbage either."

Ian scooped out servings of the food onto his own plate. "Well, there's nothing like the smell of a cabbage boiling," he said.

Mary wrinkled her nose as she carried her plate over to the table. "Yes, we can agree on that."

He laughed and followed her over. "And now that we've finished discussing food, what are our next steps to help our ghost?"

"Do you have the yearbook?" Mary asked.

He nodded.

"Well, it can't be too hard to find a Nickolas in the yearbook," Mary said. "Let's see if we can track down the old boyfriend and see what he has to say."

Ian got up from the table and walked over to the desk. He picked up the yearbook and brought it back with him to the table. "Let's start with her class first," he said.

They started to flip through the pages when Ian, his mouth full of potatoes, stopped their progress by pounding a finger on one of the pictures.

"What is it?" Mary asked.

"Mmmpfh," Ian replied, trying to clear his mouth.

"Oh, well then, that is serious," Mary said, smiling at him.

She looked down at the photo. "Ian, that's a girl. We're looking for a boy."

"Katie," he was finally able to say. "That's Katie Brennan."

"No," Mary said, and then she bent forward and looked closer. "You're right. It is Katie. Boy, I bet she hates this picture."

Ian chortled. "Well, the eighties weren't kind to many. I wonder if she knew Hope."

"It's a small class," Mary said. "And if she didn't know Hope, I bet she'd know Nickolas."

They quickly put the food away and walked down the block to the Brennans' home. A few moments after they rang the doorbell, Katie answered the door. She was wiping her hands on a dishcloth and her house smelled like cinnamon.

"Sorry, just made some cookies and I'm cleaning up," she said, as she invited them in. "What's up?"

Ian sniffed the air. "Well, this might take a while," he said. "We might be in need of nourishment."

Katie laughed, led them into the kitchen and invited them to sit at the table. "Snickerdoodles," she said, pushing a plate piled high with cookies toward Ian. "Try one."

He winked at her. "Well, if you insist," he said, snatching a large one from the top and biting into it.

Closing his eyes as he ate, he slowly nodded his head. "Oh, yes, Katie, these are amazing."

Looking over at Katie, Mary rolled her eyes. "You would never know we just had lunch," she said. "I don't know how he eats like that and stays trim."

"It's a curse," Ian said. "A pure curse."

"Well, curse or not, we're actually here to ask you a question about a case we're working on," Mary said. "Did you know Hope or Faith Foley?"

"Wow, I haven't heard Hope's name in years," she said, shaking her head sadly. "We were all so shocked. We never even thought that she would take her life."

"Were you friends with either girl?" Ian asked.

"Yes, Faith and I were…well, not exactly friends," she admitted. "I was in choir with her and she and I were folder partners. She was actually nice to me, unlike how she was to many of the others."

"Were you friends with Hope?" Mary asked.

"No, I wasn't," she said. "They had a rivalry, and if they thought you were friends with one, the other wouldn't speak to you. It made things a little awkward in school."

"Did you know Nickolas, Hope's boyfriend?" Ian asked.

"Really? Nick liked Hope? I never knew that," she said. "But that explains a lot."

"Why?" Mary asked. "Who's Nick?"

"Nick Kazakos. He runs the cemetery at the far end of town," Katie said. "He's a real loner and has been angry for a long time."

"Angry, like kill people kind of angry?" Mary asked.

"No," Katie responded instantly. "He doesn't seem dangerous, just sad. Intensely sad."

"Like someone who lost their one true love?" Ian asked.

Nodding, Katie turned to Ian. "Exactly."

"Did you know any of the girls who killed themselves later?" Mary asked.

"Yes, I knew them all," she admitted. "And once again, I never saw it coming. Mandy, the second girl who died, had just spoken with me at the grocery store the night before it happened."

"This might sound a wee bit odd," Ian said. "But can you remember what she was buying?"

Katie paused for a moment and thought about his request. She remembered it was near a holiday and she had been shopping late at night, at the last minute. "Yes, I do remember, because we laughed about both of us running out at the last minute to get our turkeys," she said. "Her cart was filled with Thanksgiving food. I commented that it looked like she was going to be cooking for a huge number of people and she told me her family was going to be coming."

"And then what happened?" Mary asked.

"Her family got to her house the next afternoon and found her," Katie said. "It was awful."

Mary placed her hand over Katie's. "I'm sorry, Katie."

She took a deep breath and wiped a tear from her eye. "It was a long time ago," she said. "But it really makes me aware…"

She paused as the door burst open and her children ran into the house. She got up to meet them at the door, but halfway there she turned back to Mary, aware she had left off mid-sentence. "I'm sorry," she laughed. "The kids come in and I forget everything I'm doing. It really makes me aware of how horrible bullying can be."

Maggie, standing in front of her mother, gasped at her mother's words and then looked past her to Mary and Ian. "How did you find out?" she asked. "I didn't mean it. I was just angry."

"Didn't mean what, Maggie?" Katie asked.

"I was mean to Clarissa today," she confessed. "I told her she was still 'dopted. I told her Bradley wasn't her daddy and everyone was just being nice to her 'cause she was an orphan."

"Maggie, I can't believe you would say that!" Katie exclaimed. "Clarissa is your friend. She has gone through so much. How could you hurt her like this?"

Mary and Ian rose from the table and walked toward the door. "We'd better get home and see how Clarissa is doing," Mary said. "Thanks for your time, Katie."

Maggie turned, tears streaming down her cheeks, and ran to Mary. "I'm so sorry," she cried. "Will you still be my friend?"

Mary knelt down next to Maggie and put her hands on her shoulders. "Maggie, I'm disappointed in you," she said. "What you did was hurtful and Clarissa needs friends right now. I will always be your friend. But I think you should be worrying about your friendship with Clarissa, not me."

Maggie nodded. "Can I come over and say sorry?" she asked.

"Why don't you come over in an hour," Mary suggested, "after we have some time to talk with her. Okay?"

Maggie nodded. "Okay."

Ian and Mary arrived back at the house just as Bradley's cruiser was pulling up to the driveway. He stopped the car and Clarissa jumped out and ran into the house without greeting any of them.

"I don't know what's going on," Bradley said, as he walked toward Mary and Ian. "She seemed angry when I picked her up and didn't say a word to me all the way home."

"She gave me the cold shoulder after recess," Mike said. "Didn't talk to me all the way home."

"I think her little heart was given a bruising today at school," Ian said.

"I'll talk to her," Mary suggested. "Ian, why don't you fill Bradley and Mike in on the rest?"

Chapter Twenty-six

Mary followed Clarissa into the house, pretending she didn't realize anything was wrong.

"How was school?" she asked, as she slipped her coat off, hung it in the closet and walked into the kitchen.

Clarissa was sitting at the kitchen table, her backpack open and homework in front of her. "Fine," she said softly.

"Good," she said. "It must be a little strange to be back in school in Freeport."

She reached for a cup and plate from the cupboard and proceeded to fill the glass with milk and make a peanut butter and jelly sandwich. "Anything interesting happen today?"

Clarissa paused, remembering her argument with Maggie and the man in the playground. But she wasn't ready to share that information. "No," she said, with a quick shake of her head.

"Ah, well, good," Mary said, carrying the treat over to the table and placing it next to the little girl.

She pulled out a chair and sat down next to her. "I had to go over to the Brennans' this afternoon," she said conversationally. "I was there when Maggie got home."

Clarissa reached over and picked up one of the four sections of the sandwich. She took a small bite and ignored Mary's comment.

"Yes, Maggie seemed pretty upset," Mary continued. "She realized she had been jealous and it caused her to say some things to a good friend. Things that weren't true."

Putting down the sandwich, Clarissa glanced up at Mary. "Weren't true?"

Mary shook her head. "Not even close to being true," she replied, looking directly into Clarissa's eyes.

Both of Clarissa's hands dropped into her lap and she stared off into the corner of the room. "Why didn't he keep me?" she whispered hoarsely. "Why didn't he want me?"

Her heart breaking, she forced herself to not gather the little girl up in her arms. Clarissa needed truth, not comfort.

"Your daddy, Bradley, was so excited to know that he and your mom were going to have you," she said. "The last time he saw you was in an ultrasound at the doctor's office. You were still inside your mom, not ready to come out yet. But they could see you were a little girl, so they stopped at the paint store and bought pink paint for your room."

Mary paused for a moment, remembering her experiences of living through Jeannine. She took a deep breath and continued. "Then an awful thing happened. A very bad man took your mommy and kept her away from your daddy. She tried to leave, tried to escape, but she couldn't. Your daddy searched and searched for both of you for a very long time. The bad man brought your mommy to another hospital, far away from your daddy, when you were born. Something happened and your mommy died at the hospital. The bad man gave you away. That's how Becca and Henry were able to adopt you. But your dad kept searching and searching for you. He just finally found out what happened to you."

"He really wants me?" she asked carefully.

Mary nodded. "One of the things that showed me how much he wanted you was when he was searching for you, when he was doing all he could to figure out where you and your mommy had gone, instead of sleeping at night, he would go into your nursery and paint it. He wanted to be sure you had a pink bedroom when he finally found you and brought you home."

A small smile grew on her face. "He did that? For me?"

"Oh, sweetheart, he never ever stopped searching for you," she said. "Even though he never got to hold you or even see you when you were born, he always loved you. And he always will."

The door opened and Bradley, Mike and Ian walked in. Bradley hurried across the room and knelt down next to Clarissa, placing one hand on the back of her chair and the other on the table in front of her. "Clarissa," he said softly. "I'm so sorry Maggie hurt your feelings today."

She launched herself into his arms and flung her arms around his neck. "I thought you didn't want me," she whispered against his shoulder.

He kissed her head and hugged her. "Oh, Clarissa, I can't begin to tell you how much I love you," he said. "But I promise I will spend the rest of my life showing you."

She nodded.

"But there's one thing you have to promise me," he continued.

She stepped back and looked at him. "'Kay," she said.

"You have to promise me that when you are troubled or hurt or even confused you come and talk to me or talk to Mary," he said. "Unless you tell us how you are feeling, we can't help you feel better."

"But Maggie said you were lying to me," she replied. "She said you were just saying stuff to be nice to me."

"I don't think lying is nice or right," he said to her. "I won't lie to you, Clarissa. If you ask me a question, I will tell you the truth."

She looked over her shoulder at Mary and then back at Bradley. "Why did you paint my room?" she asked.

He gathered her back up in his arms and cleared his throat before he could speak. Mary could see the moisture gather in his eyes.

"I painted your room because I hoped that I would find you and I wanted everything to be perfect for you when you came home," he said. "And I promised your mother that she would have a pink nursery for her little girl."

"My mommy wanted pink too?" she asked.

Nodding, he lifted her back up into her chair. "She wanted you dressed in pink from head to toe, she wanted you to have a pink stroller, a pink carseat, a pink bed and she even tried to talk me into painting the whole house pink, just for you."

Clarissa laughed. "I do like pink," she confessed.

He reached up and cupped her cheek in his hand. "So did your mother," he said.

Clarissa turned to Mary. "Do you like pink?" she asked.

"I do," she said, "but maybe not as much as your mom."

The doorbell rang and Ian hurried over to answer it. Maggie stood on the doorstep and looked into the room. "Can I come in?" she asked, her eyes already red with sorrow.

"Aye, you can," Ian said.

"Maggie, I think you have some apologizing to do," Mike said.

She nodded and started forward until she saw Bradley. Then she froze in her steps and tears formed in her eyes. Bradley stood up and walked over to her. Maggie's eyes followed him and she gulped when he stood towering over her. "Maggie, I'm glad you came," he said, "and after you talk with Clarissa, I'd like to speak to you."

Eyes as wide as saucers, she bobbed her head up and down, she slipped past him and hurried over to Clarissa.

Mary joined the men near the staircase, so the two girls could have their privacy.

"I'll go upstairs and see if I can't make myself busy for a while," Ian said with a sympathetic smile and then he whispered to Bradley, "Don't be too hard on the lass, she's feeling a wee bit replaced."

Bradley nodded in agreement. "Yes, I know," he whispered back. "I won't terrorize her, I promise."

"Aye, then I'm off," Ian replied. "Call me when it's safe to come down."

In a few minutes, the girls were laughing and hugging each other. It seemed to the adults standing by the door that the issues had been resolved and their feelings were confirmed when Clarissa looked over at them, smiling broadly and said, "We're still the 'doption girls, 'cept we're going to have a new name."

"That's a great idea," Mary said. "What's your new name?"

Clarissa and Maggie glanced at each other and giggled. "Mike's girls," they said together.

Mike grinned broadly. "I think that's the best name I've ever heard."

"That's great," Bradley agreed. "But now Maggie and I need to have a conversation."

"Uh, oh," Clarissa said.

"Come on, Clarissa," Mary said. "Let's go upstairs so you can change your clothes."

"Do you want me to stay?" Mike asked.

Bradley shook his head. "No, this is just between Maggie and me," he said.

When they were alone, Bradley walked over and sat down at the kitchen table next to Maggie. The chair scraped the floor as he pulled it out and Maggie jumped in her chair.

"There's nothing to be nervous about," Bradley said. "I just wanted to clear some things up between us."

She nodded her head, but kept her eyes focused on the table.

"Maggie, you have played such an important part in my life and in Clarissa's life," he said. "I just wanted to thank you and let you know that you will always hold a special place in my heart."

Her head jerked up and she stared at him. "What?"

"You helped Clarissa when she lived here in Freeport by telling her what her mom wanted her to know," he said. "And then you told Mary and me about her, so we could find her. You helped us save Clarissa. We couldn't have done it without you."

"You couldn't?" she asked.

He shook his head. "No, you are a very important part of our team," he said. "You're like part of our family – just like Ian and Mike are. I hope you always remember that."

"I'm part of your team?" she asked.

He nodded. "Oh, yes, you're very important to us and I will never forget how much I owe you for what you did."

She looked back at the table for a moment. "I thought you'd forget about me, 'cause you had Clarissa."

Bradley put his hand on Maggie's shoulder and waited until she looked up at him. "Maggie, I could never forget about you," he said.

"Are you mad at me?" she asked.

"No, I'm not mad," he replied. "But I really didn't like what you said to Clarissa. It made her sad. And if we're a team, we shouldn't make each other sad. We should be working hard to make each other happy."

She nodded. "I'll work hard to make us happy," she said. "And I won't make Clarissa sad, so she never talks to the strange man in the playground ever again."

Bradley froze. "What strange man?"

Chapter Twenty-seven

"Clarissa!" Bradley called from the bottom of the stairs.

Mary and Mike looked at each other from across Clarissa's room.

"He doesn't sound very happy," Clarissa said, as she closed her dresser drawer.

Mary shook her head. "No, he doesn't," she said, as she picked up Clarissa's coat and began to hang it up. "He almost sounds…"

She stopped as an envelope fell out of the pocket on to the floor. She bent to pick it up and saw it was addressed to Bradley. "What's this?" she asked Clarissa.

"Ohhhhhh," she replied.

Mary walked back across the room, leaving the coat lying over a chair. "Oh?"

"A strange man talked to me at recess," she said. "And he told me to give the letter to my daddy."

"When did that happen?" Mike asked. "Where was I?"

"You were talking to Maggie," Clarissa explained. "He was only there for a few minutes."

"I can't believe I didn't see him," Mike said.

Mary put her arm around Clarissa's shoulders. "Well, let's go downstairs and give this to you daddy," she said. "I have a feeling it's not going to make him much happier."

They met Bradley at the foot of the stairs. "Where's Maggie?" Clarissa asked.

"I walked her home," Bradley said. "She had homework to do. But she told me that at recess you walked away from her and spoke to a strange man."

Clarissa nodded her head. "When I was mad at Maggie, I walked away to the other side of the playground. A man was on the other side of the fence and he talked to me."

"What did he say to you?" Bradley asked, his heart pounding.

"He gave her this letter," Mary interjected.

Bradley looked up, surprised. "You knew?"

Mary shook her head. "No, I just found the letter when I was hanging up her coat," she replied. "She forgot about it with all of the problems with Maggie."

Bradley took the letter from Mary and held it over a lamplight. "There doesn't seem to be anything in it but paper," he said.

"Oh, I hadn't even thought…" Mary said, chastising herself mentally.

"Do you have any gloves?" Bradley asked.

"Ian does," she said.

She called up to Ian and he quickly came down carrying a pair of latex gloves. "What's going on?" he asked.

"A strange man spoke with Clarissa in the schoolyard," Mike said. "He gave her a letter for Bradley."

"You've checked it for chemical agents?" Ian asked.

"I held it over the light," Bradley said. "There doesn't seem to be anything inside but paper."

"Aye, but if you think we're dealing with Gary Copper, he's a mite smarter about his poisons," he said. "It might not be a powder. It could be something sprayed on the paper."

"What are you thinking?" Mary asked.

Ian shrugged. "Well, if I was wanting someone to die a slow and painful – though hard to detect – death, I might consider ricin."

Bradley dropped the envelope on the table and stepped back. "Okay, Professor, you're the expert. What's next?"

Ian slipped on the gloves and picked up the envelope. He turned it around and examined it. "You'll note that he took the time to not only seal the envelope, but also to tape it over," he said. "So it wouldn't be easy for Clarissa to open it and check what's inside. My best guess is that if there is poison, it would be inside the envelope. But we might be able to see if there are traces on the outside."

"Shouldn't we call someone?" Mary asked.

"Well, not until we're sure," Ian said. "We just have to do a quick fluorescence to see if we can pick anything up."

"A quick fluorescence?" Mike asked. "What the hell is that?"

"Angels aren't supposed to say that word," Clarissa corrected.

"Sorry, sweetheart," Mike replied. "What the *heck* is that?"

"Come on up to my laboratory," he said, "I'll show you."

He led them upstairs to his bedroom. Mary was shocked to see the variety of electronic equipment sitting on folding tables throughout the room. There were computers attached to other machines attached to control boards attached to monitors.

"So this is why the electric bill has hit the roof," she said, looking around. "And I thought it was because I left my curling iron on."

He grinned at her. "Don't worry, darling, I'll reimburse you."

Hurrying across the room to one of the desks, he pressed a button and the lid of a plastic box opened with a hiss, breaking the airtight seal. He placed the envelope inside the box and sealed it tightly.

Pulling up a chair next to the desk, he opened another smaller box that was situated next to the first one. A small round tube connected the boxes together, creating an airway between them. Halfway up the wall of the second box was a small plastic bowl, attached by an axle to a lever on the outside. Ian opened a dark-colored bottle and poured liquid into the bottom of the small box. Then he opened a metal container and carefully scooped out a small amount of the powder inside and placed it in the bowl. He closed the container and then sealed the lid of the box.

When he turned the lever, the powder fell down onto the liquid and immediately a gas cloud formed inside the chamber and moved through the tube into the plastic box containing the envelope.

"This is what we call the immunoassay," Ian said. "The chemical in the chamber floats over to the box and binds itself to the chemical on the envelope. Then the magic happens."

"Magic?" Clarissa asked.

He winked at her. "Yeah, magic," he said. "Mary would you be a dear and close the door and turn out the light."

The room was dark for a moment and then Ian reached over and turned on a machine next to the box. The green readout numbers glowed in the dark room. Ian adjusted a few knobs and a moment later the envelope began to glow.

"We have a winner," Ian whispered. "There is a strong possibility of ricin in the envelope. Now it's time to call in your friends from the Health Department to get a hazmat team out here."

Bradley pulled out his radio-phone and made the call.

Mary's heart dropped and she hurried over to Ian. "What about Clarissa? She's had that envelope in her pocket all afternoon."

Ian turned to her. "There's just a trace amount on the envelope," he said, "just enough to implicate the contents, not enough to do her any harm. Inhaling ricin is generally what kills people. It's highly unlikely to absorb it through the skin."

She relaxed and allowed her heart to return to normal for a moment. "He wanted to kill Bradley," she said.

"That or scare him," Ian agreed.

"Like the phone call," she said.

"What phone call?" Bradley asked, as he hung up the phone.

"Crap," Mary whispered.

She turned to Bradley. "There was a message on my office phone from Gary," she said.

"And you didn't call me immediately because...?" he asked.

"I didn't think it was important enough to bother you," she said.

Bradley turned away from her and stared at the small glowing particles on the envelope. He knew he was angry and he was frightened. *Gary Copper was within touching distance of Clarissa today. He could have just as easily shot her as handed her this envelope.* He dragged his hand through his hair. *And Mary! Didn't want to bother me! What the hell did she think was more important to me than her safety?* He took several deep breaths, but it didn't work this time. This time it was too important and this time he was too emotionally involved.

152

He turned back and looked directly into Mary's eyes. "I need to go downstairs and meet the hazmat team," he said. "When I get back, we'll talk."

She nodded, feeling a pit grow in the middle of her stomach. "Bradley, I…"

Holding up his hand, he stopped. "Not now, Mary," he said. "Please, just give me a little time to be able to think clearly."

He turned to Ian. "Clarissa?"

"She's fine, Bradley," he assured her. "There wasn't enough on the envelope to do her harm, but I'll help Mary and we'll wash her up."

Finally, he knelt down next to Clarissa. "How are you?" he asked.

"I'm sorry I made you angry," she replied.

Sighing slowly, he pulled her against him and hugged her. "I'm not angry with you," he said. "I was worried because that man could have hurt you and I don't want anything to happen to you. Do you understand?"

She nodded against him. "I won't ever go by the playground fence again," she promised. "And I'll never, ever talk to the strange man again."

"Thank you, sweetheart," he said. "Now go with Ian and Mary."

He stood up, turned away from Mary and left the room.

"He's pretty mad at you," Clarissa said, as they listened to him walk down the stairs.

Mary nodded slowly. "Yes, I think he is," she replied.

153

"'Cause he worries about you too?" she asked.

"Yes, that's exactly why," she replied. "And he wants to protect us."

"That's good, right?" Clarissa asked.

Smiling ruefully, Mary nodded. "Yes, sweetheart, that's good."

Chapter Twenty-eight

The leader of the hazmat team was actually a man Mike had worked with years ago at the fire department. "We used to call him Meticulous Matt," Mike said. "This guy follows the book completely and does a good job."

He came up the stairs, dressed in his hazmat equipment, and met with Ian who explained the test he ran on the envelope. Matt took detailed notes and finally, once Ian had explained everything asked, "And what are you doing with this kind of equipment in a residential home?"

"Yep, this is where Scottie tells them he's a ghostbuster and has ectoplasm in his closet," Mike said to Mary and Clarissa.

Clarissa giggled and Mike winked at her. Ian coughed, hiding his grin and turned back to the team. "I'm a professor from the University of Edinburgh. I'm here doing research through a fellowship with the University of Chicago," he explained. "This is the equipment I need for testing and supporting my thesis."

"What is the thesis about?" Matt asked.

"Oh, come on, Matt," Mike groaned. "I went to school with you, buddy. The only deep educational pursuits you had were classic graphic novels and that's only because the babes were hot. Who are you trying to kid?"

Ian had to cough again. "Aye, well it's about preternatural phenomenon and electromagnetic residue," he finally was able to say. "Have you heard of it?"

"Ian's very smart," Clarissa said.

Matt shrugged. "Yeah, it sounds familiar."

Mike hooted and shook his head. "Yeah, like Einstein's theory sounds familiar."

"We'd like your permission to remove the envelope within the plastic casing," Matt said.

"Oh, of course," Ian agreed. "That's the safest way to get the envelope out of here. Once you decontaminate it, I'd like it back."

"No problem," Matt agreed. "Were there any other areas contaminated?"

"Well, Clarissa carried the envelope home in her coat pocket," Mary volunteered. "Ian suggested I double bag it for you to take."

"I'm going to get a new coat," Clarissa volunteered. "Mary said so."

Matt looked down at Clarissa. "That's great, thank you for giving us your old coat," Matt said, and then he smiled at Mary. "You've done a great job, ma'am."

"Too bad, Ian," Mike added. "Guess you're not cute enough to have done a good job."

Giggling again, Clarissa clapped her hands over her mouth.

Matt turned to Ian. "We'd also like to take the gloves you used," he said. "Is there anything else that came in contact with the envelope?"

"The table downstairs," Ian said, "and I believe Bradley cleaned it thoroughly."

"Chief Alden has also opened all of the windows downstairs to air the house out," Matt said.

"And we've cleaned any skin that came into contact with the envelope. Mostly on Clarissa and Mary," Ian added.

"Should we find another place to spend the night?" Mary asked.

Matt smiled at her. "No, I'm sure you'll be safe," he said. "The amount of exposure was really minimal."

"Thank you so much," Mary replied, smiling back at him.

"No...no problem," he said. "If I can be of any more help...if you need anything..."

"And Mary O'Reilly has once again devastated a man with her smile," Mike said.

"Mary is going to marry my daddy, Bradley," Clarissa inserted protectively.

"Oh," Matt's smile fell. "Well, congratulations."

"Thank you," Mary replied, putting her arm around Clarissa's shoulders.

"Good job, sweetheart," Mike added.

Clarissa winked at Mike.

After finishing all of the steps in their protocol, the team met with everyone in the living room. "It looks like you've done everything correctly," Matt said. "We'll conduct more tests on the envelope and get back to you, Chief Alden."

"Thank you," he said. "And it's important that any message or fingerprints from the envelope are preserved for further investigation and possible indictment."

"Yes, sir, we'll remember to treat this as evidence," Matt assured him.

"Thanks for your good work," Bradley said, as he escorted them to the door. "I'll be in touch with you in the morning."

He turned back to the room and his eyes met Mary's. "We should talk," he said.

"Aye, you should," Ian said. "But the department store will be closing in thirty minutes and Clarissa is going to need a coat in the morning."

Mary nodded. "Why don't we go get the coat," she said. "We can talk on the way."

"And I'll order pizza for delivery," Ian added. "We'll keep some warm for you."

"Thanks, Ian," Mary said, and went over to the kitchen table to get her coat.

Bradley reached for his coat in the closet and then stopped and turned to Ian. "Where are you going to order pizza from?" he asked. "Do you know the delivery person?"

"I'll order from Joe's," he said. "I know the delivery man. He's come here a number of times."

He held up his hand to stave off another question from Bradley. "But not enough times to have become routine for anyone watching the house," he added quickly.

Bradley released a long, slow breath. "Thanks, Ian," he said. "I'll try not to continue to be paranoid."

"You've got a good reason to be careful," Ian said, "and we would all be wise to be a bit more paranoid."

Chapter Twenty-nine

Mary and Bradley walked out to his cruiser in silence. He opened the door for her and she slipped in. Once he got into the car, he turned it on, but didn't put the car in drive. He sat in the seat, his hands on the steering wheel, staring out the front window. "Mary, I realize…"

"Bradley, I'm sorry," she interrupted. "I should have called you."

He nodded, but didn't turn toward her. "Why didn't you?" he asked softly.

She didn't have to think about her answer for long, she had asked herself that same question all night long. "His call got to me," she said quietly. "His voice terrified me. I literally got sick when I heard his message."

Turning to her, his eyes were filled with confusion. "I don't understand," he said. "Isn't that when you should have come to me?"

Would he? Could he understand when she was having a hard time totally understanding it herself?

"I don't want to be terrified anymore," she explained. "I don't want to be weak. I don't want to give him that kind of power over me. After I got sick, I got mad. Really mad. I wanted to kick his butt. And it felt…"

She paused and met his eyes, praying that he would understand. "And it felt like going to you right away was admitting defeat. Was like running off to someone else who could and would take care of me, instead of taking care of myself. I didn't want to let him win again."

Bradley released his hold on the steering wheel and sat back in his seat. "We're a team, Mary," he finally said.

She turned in her seat, facing him. "Yes, we are," she agreed. "And I brought the answering machine home, so you could hear it. And I was going to share every detail with you. But I couldn't go running to you right away, like a scared child."

"I can understand that," he replied, turning toward her.

"And if I had any idea that he had made that call from town, that he'd been in contact with Clarissa…" She bent her head. "I would not have done anything to risk her safety."

He leaned over, caressing her cheek with his hand and finally cupping her chin and gently turning her to face him. "I know that," he said. "I know you'd lay down your life for her."

She met his eyes. "She means the world to you…to us."

Nodding, he smiled slightly as he ran his thumb over her lips. "She's not the only one who means the world to me."

Smiling tremulously, she nodded. "Yeah, for me too," she replied. "I'm sorry I made you angry."

Chuckling, as he realized Mary had just repeated the same words Clarissa had used, he leaned over and placed a gentle kiss on her lips. "With two women in my household, I'm never going to win, right?" he asked, his face just inches from hers.

She slid her hands up his neck and buried her fingers in his hair. With a twinkle in her eyes, she smiled at him and just before she pulled his face closer for a deeper kiss, she whispered, "Not a chance."

Chapter Thirty

"This reminds me of walking through the moors at home," Ian said, as he and Mary walked across the grounds of the cemetery in the early morning fog.

"This reminds me of an old Sherlock Holmes movie," Mary said. "And at any moment, the Hounds of Baskerville are going to come charging out from behind one of these tombstones."

"Aye, as I said, just like home," he teased.

Laughing, she looked around them and shivered just a little. The temperature had warmed considerably and the difference between the frozen ground and warm air had caused a fog so thick that visibility was considered zero. They had taken their time driving the few blocks to the cemetery and found a note on the door that the owner was on the grounds. So they decided to take a walk and find him.

Fog literally rolled across the ground, hiding tombstones and sepulchers until you were right next to them, and then they would appear out of the mist as a stone ghost. Even sounds were muffled by the fog, creating a feeling of complete isolation.

"This is kind of creepy," Mary admitted.

"Have I ever told you my theory about zombies?" Ian asked conversationally. "That I found some evidence that they actually might exist?"

"Really? You had to bring that up here? Now?"

They passed a crypt the size of a large garden shed and they both jumped when the life-sized stone angel guarding it seemed to come out of nowhere.

"If that had been a zombie, your brain would have been breakfast," Mary said.

"Not if she caught you first," he argued.

"Oh, and here I was under the impression that you would throw yourself into the zombie's arms and tell me to run and save myself," she teased.

"Mary, darling, you know I'd do that normally," he replied, "but since I might be the only one with the key to saving the entire human race, I'm afraid I'd have to trip you and run."

She started to laugh and then froze. Ian paused next to her and they both listened to the soft thudding sound in the distance.

"What do you think it is?" she whispered.

Ian listened for another moment. "If I'm not mistaking, someone is digging out here."

"But don't they use backhoes to dig new gravesites?" she asked.

"Perhaps they're not digging up a new one," he suggested. "Perhaps they're reacquainting themselves with an old friend."

She turned to him. "I really should go walking in the fog with you more often. I've seen a whole other side to your personality."

The rhythmic thudding continued and, as they got closer, they could pick out the sound of metal occasionally scraping against rock.

"My money's on digging," Mary whispered.

"Do you want to know what I think?" Ian whispered back.

Mary paused and turned to him. "No, I really don't."

Ian grinned and they continued toward the sound. The fog seemed to thicken as they got closer, rolling like great puffs of steam that encompassed the world around them. "We must be going downhill," he whispered. "Fog collects in low spots."

Nodding wordlessly, Mary strained her ears to hear.

Suddenly, Ian stumbled on a loose rock and sent it clattering ahead of them.

"Who's there?" a man's voice called out into the fog.

"Um, hello," Mary said in her friendliest voice. "I'm looking for Nick."

"Who are you?" Nick asked, his voice laced with distrust.

Mary continued to move toward the voice. "I'm sorry," she said, trying to buy a little more time. "What did you ask?"

"I want to know who you are and why you are looking for me?" he growled back.

Mary and Ian walked over a slight rise and caught sight of a slender man. He was standing near a large oak tree with a shovel in his hands, held like a quarterstaff, ready to do battle. The fog rolled around him, nearly obscuring his features from them. They could see the ground beneath had been freshly dug and hastily covered.

"Hello, Nick?" Mary asked as she tentatively moved closer.

"Who the hell are you?" he asked, his voice slightly high pitched, like he hadn't really moved on past puberty.

"My name is Mary," she replied as she moved even closer. "Mary O'Reilly. And this is my friend, Professor Ian MacDougal. We are doing some research and we were told you might be able to help us."

He turned the shovel and thrust it into the ground next to him. "Help you with what?"

Since he was more or less disarmed, they both walked up next to him. Ian looked down at the overturned dirt and saw the flattened earth around the small section of freshly turned ground. He looked up at the man's face. Nick's face was slightly flushed and, even in the cool fog, he had worked up a sweat. "Did your pet die?" Ian asked.

"How did you...?" he paused, wiping the sweat from his brow. "Have you been spying on me?"

Ian shook his head. "Oh, no," he said, shrugging his shoulders. "I've a large place back home in Scotland and we've quite a family of cats. I'm fond of them and whenever one of them passes, I take it upon myself to see they've been cared for properly. I've dug many a small grave in the wee hours of the morning."

Nick shrugged. "Wasn't even my cat," he said. "Some idiot ran it over this morning. Left it in the gutter to die like it was a piece of trash. Didn't even stop."

"Perhaps they didn't see it," Mary offered.

"Yeah, right," Nick scoffed. "More likely they didn't want to waste their time on something they considered beneath them. Assholes."

"Do they let you bury animals in the cemetery next to people?" Mary asked.

Nick stared at Mary for a moment. "Nope, they don't," he said. "You gonna turn me in?"

"All I've seen is some loose dirt," she replied. "Isn't that a common occurrence at a cemetery?"

He nodded slowly, his scowl lightening a little. "Yeah, I guess it is. Besides, they deserve a proper burial more than most of the folks buried here."

"You don't like people much, do you, Nick?" Ian asked.

His mouth turned up in a slight sneer and he met Ian's eyes. "I like them best when I can put them six feet under," he said. "They don't bother me then."

"Have you always felt this way about people?" Mary asked. "Or did it happen after Hope died?"

His eyes flashed with anger. "How do you know about Hope?"

167

"We're actually investigating her death," Mary said. "Her mother mentioned you to us."

His laughter was bitter and quick. "Oh, yeah, and I bet she used the most flattering terms when she mentioned me," he said. "Did she tell you I was a foreigner?"

Ian nodded. "She might have mentioned that."

"My family has been here in Freeport for four generations," he said. "My great-grandfather arrived here after World War I, but to someone like her, we will always be foreigners."

"Did she oppose your relationship with Hope?" Mary asked.

"No, she didn't give a damn about Hope," he said. "But if I'd been interested in Faith, well, that would have been a whole different story."

"Why?" Ian asked. "They were both her daughters."

Nick lifted the shovel and shoved it back into the ground. "Hope was not quite…as acceptable as Faith," he said angrily, his protruding Adam's apple bobbing with emotion. "She was a little heavier, her skin wasn't as perfect and she wasn't the cheerleader type. Instead she was kind, sensitive and bright. Not the right temperament for the Foley family."

"Why do you think she killed herself?" Mary asked.

He looked out into the fog for a moment and then inhaled deeply. "They must have done something to her," he finally said. "They must have

168

said something or done something. She would have never… She wasn't planning…"

He picked up the shovel and slammed it against the tree. Mary and Ian jumped back.

"Damn it, she had just told me she loved me," he said. "You don't say that and then kill yourself. She had too much to live for."

"Did you…were you anywhere near the house on the night it happened?" Ian asked.

"We were supposed to meet, after the lights went out," he said. "I waited. I waited for her. I saw the light in her room go on. Then I heard the ambulance…"

He thrust the shovel into the ground again. "I was right outside," he said, his teeth clenched. "All she had to do was come outside. We could have run away together… Why the hell did she leave me?"

"Why did she leave you?" Mary asked. "Didn't she leave you a note?"

He shook his head. "No, no note. When I asked about her, her family told me to leave and never come back. I didn't even get to go to her funeral. They only allowed the family."

"None of her friends attended the funeral?" Ian asked.

Nick shook his head. "No. The only ones at the funeral were Mr. and Mrs. Foley. Faith was already gone. They sent her to Europe. She probably didn't want to attend anyway."

"Has she ever spoken about it?" Mary asked.

"Listen, Faith and I don't run in the same circles," Nick replied. "I haven't seen Faith since the day Hope died."

"You saw Faith the day Hope died?" Ian asked. "Why?"

Nick's face flushed and he turned away for a moment. "She asked me to meet her," he finally said.

"Why?" Mary asked.

He kicked at the ground for a moment, and then looked up and met Mary's eyes. "Because I was an idiot."

"I don't understand," she replied.

"Faith was beautiful," he said resentfully. "She looked like she just stepped out of a magazine. Tall, thin, nicely built, long straight hair, white straight teeth – she was the whole package. Well, on the outside. The inside was not as nice."

"I still don't get it."

"She flirted with me," he yelled. "She told me she thought I was cute. Said she thought nerdy guys were hot."

"She was setting you up," Ian said.

Nick nodded. "Yeah, she met me behind the school, got me hot and bothered and timed it just perfectly."

"Hope?" Mary asked.

"Hope found us kissing," he said. "She ran away crying."

He looked away from them. "I turned to Faith and she was laughing. She was watching her sister run away, broken hearted, and she was laughing.

Then she turned and walked away from me," he said, then he turned back to face them. "She had done what she'd set out to do. She might as well have put the cord around Hope's neck. She killed her sister. She was nothing but a bitch then and I'm sure she's the same now."

Chapter Thirty-one

"I don't think he killed Hope or witnessed her death," Ian said once he and Mary were back in the car together.

"Yes, I agree," she said. "But I wouldn't rule him out as the person seeking revenge on those who made fun of her."

Mary turned the car on and slowly pulled out into the street. "So you don't think the deaths of the other women were suicides?" Ian asked.

Shaking her head, she kept her eyes on the foggy road ahead of her. "No, but right now it's just a hunch. Katie was right, people who are contemplating suicide aren't planning for the holidays," she said. "I think we need to get some more information on their deaths."

"Okay, we could start with the police reports," Ian suggested. "I know it would make a certain police chief really happy if you were working nearby."

She turned and smiled at him. "I think you're right," she agreed. "Should we swing by Cole's and get doughnuts before we go there?"

"You know the whole doughnut-eating police officer is an overused stereotype," Ian said. "Not all police officers like pastries."

Mary nodded. "Okay, I can agree with that," she paused for a moment. "So, are we picking up doughnuts?"

Waiting just a beat to answer, Ian smiled at her and nodded. "Aye, we are."

Once they arrived at the station, they dropped the doughnuts off at the front desk and knocked on the door to the Chief's office. "Come in," Bradley called from inside the room.

Mary opened the door and peeked inside. Bradley was at his desk, reviewing some paperwork. "Good morning," she said.

He immediately lifted his head and smiled at her. "Now it is," he said, getting out of his chair and walking to the door. "Come in."

Mary and Ian both entered. "Ian and I wanted to look over the police reports on the other girls that committed suicide."

"Aye, we thought it would be better to start here than try to interview their relatives," Ian added. "Their comments back then are probably more relevant."

"That's a good idea," Bradley agreed. "Do you know where the record room is?"

"Yes, just down the hall," Ian said. "I'll head over there now and give you two a couple of minutes."

Ian pulled the door closed behind him as Bradley stepped over and slipped his arms around Mary's waist and she folded her arms around his neck. "Good morning," he said quietly, bringing his lips down to hers.

"Now it is," she murmured with a smile as she returned the kiss, feeling the slow burn in her abdomen as she tightened her arms to deepen the kiss.

He kissed her again, first gently, exploring her taste, enjoying her response and responding to her soft murmurs and sighs. Then he let his desire take the reins as he crushed her lips beneath his and pulled her closer. She reacted with an answering passion and kissed him back, breathing in short staccato bursts as her heart pounded in her chest, moaning in frustration as she felt the tension build inside of her.

Bradley drew back and nearly lost all control when he looked down at her kiss-swollen lips, her face flushed with passion and her eyes soft with desire. "Mary," he whispered, his voice hoarse with emotion. "I think we'd better slow things down."

In an emotionally-charged daze, she nodded at him and tightened her arms to continue the kiss.

He ducked around her luscious lips and kissed her neck, which caused her to shiver deliciously in his arms. "Darling, unless we stop, we're going to have to move the wedding up to yesterday," he whispered into her ear.

She paused, confused. "Yesterday? I don't understand..."

The sensual fog she was in had been even more powerful than the fog she had walked in that morning. But suddenly it lifted away and Mary looked up at Bradley, his eyes still filled with desire and tenderness.

"You pack a punch," he said, smiling down at her.

"You're not so bad yourself," she replied, still trying to catch her breath.

"How many months until we get married?" he asked, placing a kiss on her forehead.

She shook her head. "Please don't ask me to do math right now," she complained. "I'll be lucky if I can think straight for the next hour."

Chuckling, he ran his hands up her arms and rested them on her shoulders. "I have that problem whenever I'm in the same room with you."

She smiled at him. "Really? I think I like that."

"It doesn't bode well for anyone relying on me to solve a crime, though," he said.

She reached up and kissed him quickly on the lips. "Well, then, I'd better let you get back to keeping Freeport safe," she replied. "And I'll go help Ian solve a mystery."

"If you need anything…" he began.

"I know where you are," she interrupted with a smile. "By the way, I brought in doughnuts. They're at the front desk. I had Dorothy put two of them to the side for you."

"I love you, Mary O'Reilly," he said.

"Good, because the feeling's very mutual," she replied just before she slipped out the door.

Chapter Thirty-two

Ian had acquisitioned a table in the middle of the record room and had set two chairs on one side. On the table were five sets of files, placed in separate piles and a whiteboard in the center. Mary entered the room to find Ian scribbling away on the whiteboard.

"Ah, Mary, excellent," he said, looking up when she opened the door. "I've located the files and have just started reviewing them."

"Five files?" she asked, walking forward and picking up the first file. "I thought there were only four copycat suicides."

"Yes, you're right," he agreed. "But I thought it wise to also look at the original file and see if we pick out anything we might have forgotten."

"You are brilliant," she replied. "So what have you found so far?"

He grinned up at her. "Well, I've found the files so far," he said. "And now the fun begins. Have a seat and let's begin our adventure."

She sat down in the seat next to him and shook her head. "You really like research, don't you?" she asked.

Flipping open the first folder, he glanced at her and winked. "I live for research," he said. "It's like being a detective without having to shoot people."

"There's nothing wrong with shooting people," Mary interjected, "if the situation calls for it."

He nodded. "And there you have the difference between a professor and a cop."

She opened her folder and then turned to him. "Being a cop is sexier," she said.

Cocking an eyebrow, he just looked at her.

Sighing, she nodded. "Present company excluded, of course."

Grinning, he nodded. "Of course. Now, come, come, the game is afoot."

"Oh, so you get to be Sherlock Holmes now?" she asked. "You do remember, he was the detective."

"First one with a clue gets to be Sherlock," Ian said.

"You're on," Mary agreed.

She picked up the folder that contained the information about Hope Foley's death and started reading. After a few minutes, she set the folder down and took a deep breath.

"Are you okay?" Ian asked her.

She nodded, but didn't say a word for a moment or two. "This is just so heartbreaking," she finally said, her voice thick with emotion. "When I see a ghost reenact their own death, it's pretty emotional. But I never see what happens afterward. What happens to the people who find them or the loved ones who grieve for the rest of their lives."

"It takes a while, but they learn to move forward," Ian murmured.

177

"I'm sorry, I didn't hear you," Mary said.

"Oh, nothing, just muttering," he said with a smile. "What did you find?"

She pushed the folder over to Ian. "Hope's mother, Gloria, found her. The report says she saw her hanging from the ceiling fan, ran across the room, wrapped her arms around Hope's legs and lifted her up, trying to relieve the cord's pressure from Hope's neck. It was already too late, but she wouldn't let go. She must have held her up for thirty minutes. Finally, the EMTs had to sedate her in order to get her to release her hold from her daughter."

"She was fighting for the life she thought her daughter had thrown away," Ian said.

Mary nodded. "And we know better."

"Aye, and the more we learn, the better chance we have of saving someone else."

Going back to work, they studied the files in silence for the next sixty minutes, both scribbling notes and checking back and forth between cases. Mary, chewing on the end of her pen, finally pushed the folder away from her and sat back in her chair. "They all look like viable suicides," she said. "Not one seems to be assisted."

"Aye, but none of them showed any of the telltale signs of someone who was going to attempt suicide," he said. "No hints about dying, no getting their lives in order or giving things away, no talk about how unfulfilling their lives were, none of the typical warning signs."

"Was there anything they all had in common," Mary wondered aloud, "other than being Faith's friends in high school?"

"And dying on the same day, four years apart?" Ian asked. "It doesn't seem like they had much contact with each other after that. They all led very dissimilar lives and even went to different colleges."

"So, we're back to their high school connection," she said. "Did you bring the yearbook with you?"

Ian reached over to his brown leather briefcase and extracted the book. "I thought it might come in handy," he said, handing it to her.

She sighed. "Fine, you get to be Sherlock."

Opening to the index at the end of the book, she began to look up each girl and list the page numbers next to their names. Ian scribbled them down on the whiteboard. "Well, this is interesting," he said. "They are all listed on page 256. Let's take a look."

There was a candid shot of a group of girls posing for the camera taken outside of the football field. The girls were smiling and posing for the photographer, their arms wrapped around each other's shoulders.

"Look at this," Mary said, pointing to a figure in the background of the photo.

Behind the girls, in the bleachers above them, a lone figure stood looking down on the group. Her hands were clasped on the chain link fencing that surrounded the field and her face was raw with emotion.

"Hope," Mary said.

"She looks so lonely," Ian added. "Breaks my heart just looking at her."

Ian glanced down the page and read the names on the caption. He looked up at Mary. "We've more to worry about than a lonely Hope. All but two of these girls are dead," he said, his tone serious.

"Who?"

"Faith Foley," he said slowly, "and Katie Mahoney, who is now Katie Brennan."

"The anniversary is in two days," Mary said.

"And unless we figure this out, one of those women is going to die," Ian added.

Chapter Thirty-three

Bradley knocked on the record room door before entering. "Can I disturb you for a moment?" he asked.

"We were just getting ready to come and see you," Mary said.

He looked at Mary and Ian, felt the tension in the room. "What's wrong?"

"We think Katie Brennan might be in danger," Ian said. "She's one of two girls still living from a yearbook photo where all of the other girls have committed suicide."

Shaking his head, Bradley breathed a quick sigh of relief. "Well, we don't have to worry there. Katie is not going to commit suicide."

"That's what they said about all of the other women," Mary said. "None of them seemed like the kind to commit suicide, yet they did. All on the anniversary of Hope Foley's death, four years apart."

"But Katie? We know Katie."

"We're thinking they might have been helped with their suicide attempts," Ian said. "But we haven't figured it out yet."

"Okay, what do you need from me?" he asked.

"Well, at this point, I'm not really sure," Mary said. "We're going to go over to Katie's and talk to her."

"Aye, warn her about the situation," Ian said.

Bradley walked over to the table and looked at the files. "Is anyone else in danger?" he asked.

"Yes," Mary said. "Faith Foley is also in the photo. We thought we'd go by and see her too."

"When's the anniversary?" Bradley asked.

"Two days from now," Ian replied. "We haven't much time to solve this one."

Mary saw Bradley start to speak and then hesitate, looking like he was trying to make up his mind. "Why did you stop by?" she asked.

Uncertain, he looked down at the table once more, then up at Mary and Ian. "Steve Turner from Walker Mortuary just called," he said. "They have everything ready for Becca's funeral, tomorrow. But considering…"

"No, we need to go and support Clarissa," Mary said without hesitation. "We can take the time for the funeral."

"Aye, we'll be there," Ian said. "It's important that we're there for her."

"Thank you," Bradley said. "I really appreciate it."

"I'll mention it to Katie, too," Mary said, "after we meet with her. I'm sure she and Clifford will want to attend. Besides, she'll be safer if she's with us."

"So, you and Ian are leaving?" Bradley asked.

Sighing, Mary stood up and walked over to Bradley. She reached up and kissed his cheek. "I'll be very careful," she said. "And I'll take Ian everywhere I go."

"Aye, we won't take any chances," Ian agreed.

"Do you want us to swing by the school and check on Clarissa?" she asked him.

Shaking his head, he smiled a little self-consciously. "Um, no, that's okay. I'm actually on my way over there myself."

"She'll be happy to see you," Mary said. "And I'll call if something comes up."

He put his hand on her shoulder before she could turn away. "Why don't you just make sure nothing comes up, okay?"

She grinned. "Okay."

Chapter Thirty-four

Katie Brennan opened the door and smiled brightly. "Well, this is a nice surprise," she said to Mary and Ian standing outside her door. "Come in, please."

They entered, but their neutral smiles did not reach their eyes.

"You both look very serious," she said. "What's up?"

"Can we talk to you about Hope Foley for a few minutes?" Mary asked. "It's important."

"Sure, let's sit at the kitchen table."

Ian placed the yearbook on the table and flipped the pages over until he got to the picture of the girls in front of the football stadium. "Do you remember this photo?" he asked.

Katie nodded. "Yes, we took it before the homecoming game," she replied. "I was just walking by and Faith pulled me into the photo to even things out. It was kind of fun to be included with the popular girls. Why do you ask?"

"Katie, all of the girls in the photo, except for you and Faith, have committed suicide," Mary said.

Katie stared down at the photo and studied it again. She slowly sat down in a chair. "You're right," she said. "All of these girls are dead. I hadn't realized…"

"We've studied the files, all of the deaths seem like suicides," Ian said.

"Seem? They weren't suicides?" Katie asked.

Mary shook her head. "We don't have any solid evidence, but we think they might have been murdered."

"Why? Why would anyone want to murder these girls?"

"Well, actually, Katie, the better question would be, 'Is the killer still out there looking to cross the next one off the list?'" Ian said.

"Wait. What? What do you mean?" Katie asked.

"We mean that there are only two more girls left in this photo, you and Faith," Mary said. "And we're concerned that you might be in danger."

"But, but I didn't know those girls very well," she protested. "I didn't hang around them. I was just in the picture."

"We don't know if the murderer knows that," Ian said.

"This is just crazy," Katie said. "I'm not going to commit suicide and no one is going to murder me. I'm just a mom."

Mary sat down next to her and took Katie's hands in her own. "You're probably right," Mary said. "It could be just a coincidence that this photo has all the girls who died. But just in case, we want you to be very careful these next couple of days."

"Why these next couple of days?" she asked.

"The women who die always die on the anniversary of Hope's death," Ian said. "And that's in two days."

"Two days," Katie repeated slowly. "And what should I be looking out for?"

"We don't know yet," Mary said. "We're still investigating."

"Aye, and there's a possibility the murderer will be going after Faith," Ian said. "She was also in the photo."

Katie placed her head in her hands and sat quietly for a moment, contemplating everything they had just told her. She thought about the other women. Thought about the conversation she'd had with Mandy, the day before she died. Mandy had a family. She had children who were now growing up without a mom. This was not going to happen to her.

She sat up, took a deep breath and turned to Mary and Ian. "Okay, what do I need to do to help you catch this person?" she asked.

"There's a lass," Ian said with a smile. "Let the fighting Irish part of you take over."

She was surprised; she could actually feel a smile begin on her face. "It's easier when you realize you're not just fighting for yourself, you're also fighting for your children," she said.

"Well, at this point, we just want you to take extra precaution," Mary said. "We don't know how this person gets control of these women."

"Aye, it could be drugs," Ian added. "So don't drink or eat anything that you haven't either made yourself or watched someone prepare."

Katie looked up at Ian. "Actually, I was thinking I might just stay home for the next couple of days," she said.

Mary paused for a moment and then nodded. "You know, that's actually a really good idea."

"I saw the hesitation," Katie said. "I'm a mom; we're trained to look for subtle nuances. What are you not telling me?"

"Becca's funeral is tomorrow," she replied.

Katie's face softened with regret. "Oh, that's right," she said. "Well, of course I'm coming to that."

Constantly amazed by the strength of the woman seated next to her, Mary was speechless at the simple statement of courage. She put her hand on Katie's arm. "No, Katie, you need to stay home and stay safe," she said softly.

Katie smiled at Mary. "Well, are you going to be there?" she asked.

"Of course," Mary replied.

"Where could I be safer than with you at my side?"

"Katie, I..."

Katie stood up. "No, it's settled. Though I would be obliged if you would give me a ride to the funeral. Then I don't have to worry about my brakes being cut."

"You're a brave woman," Ian said. "Have you driven with Mary before?"

"Ian," Mary chastised, standing up and slapping him lightly on his arm. "That was rude."

Katie laughed. "Okay, that felt better."

Mary turned and gave Katie a hug. "If you need anything, call me," she said. "And if you feel anything is in the least bit suspicious, call me."

"Aye, and if you are going someplace out of the ordinary, check in with us," Ian said.

"I feel like I'm sixteen again," Katie said, as she walked them to the front door.

"Well, you don't look much older than you did in the photo," Ian said. "So that's understandable."

Katie laughed again. "Well then Ian, you've just made my day. Are you going over to Faith's now?"

"Yes, we need to warn her too," Mary replied. "She wasn't very receptive when we talked to her about her sister's death earlier in the week. I hope she'll listen to us this time."

"She changed a lot after her sister's death," Katie said. "She was a different person. I heard that after Europe she went to Stanford for school. The Faith I knew could have never made it through the entrance exams. I guess having someone you love die changes your perspective on life."

"Do you think she really loved her sister?" Ian asked.

Katie nodded. "Oh, yes, even though there were issues, deep down I think there was also love."

Chapter Thirty-five

A few minutes later Mary and Ian found themselves in the same wood-paneled meeting room at the offices of Foley and Foley. Their reception this time was not as friendly and Mary had to drop Bradley's name in order to get through the door.

"I don't think we're going to get sparkling water this time," Ian said. "They don't seem very happy to see us."

"Well, perhaps we weren't as impressed with them as we should have been last time," Mary said with a smile. "We'll have to do better."

Ian laughed. "Aye, I'm used to dealing with royalty," he said. "I can flatter the best of them."

The opening of the door silenced their conversation and Faith walked in the room. She was, once again, dressed with intricate care and an eye to detail. She looked like she walked off the pages of a fashion magazine. "I understand you wanted to see me," she said.

"We have been doing some further investigation into suicides in the community and have discovered a troubling pattern," Mary said. "And we wanted to warn you."

Taken aback, Faith placed her hands on the table and leaned forward. "Who do you think you are that you can warn me about anything?" she snapped.

Calmly leaning forward, Ian shook his head. "I think you may have misunderstood our meaning, Miss Foley," he said. "We believe you to be in danger and we only want to keep you safe."

She flushed and stepped back. "Oh, of course, I'm sorry," she said. "I apologize for jumping to the wrong conclusion."

Using his most disarming manner, Ian smiled at her. "Don't worry, darling," he said. "Do you have a moment to speak with us?"

She slipped into a chair across from Ian. "Of course," she said. "Thank you."

Clasping his hands together and placing them on the table in front of him, he leaned forward slightly in his chair, meeting her eyes with his own. "The anniversary of your sister's death is this week," he said, his voice soft and comforting. "I'm sure it's hard for you."

Nodding, she fidgeted with her hair for a moment, and then finally nodded. "Yes, it is," she said. "It never seems to get easier."

"Aye," he said. "Not only did you lose your sister, but you also lost your family."

She began to argue, but he interrupted. "Your family structure, the way things operated in your home at the time," he said.

"Yes," she said. "Everything was different after she died."

"It must have been difficult to have to go away before you even had a chance to say goodbye to your sister," he added.

Tears formed in her eyes. "It was very…hard," she finished. "I felt like I lost my sister and my parents. I felt like I was blamed, in some way, for her death."

"But your parents, they were just trying to protect you," he said.

"Protect me and protect the family name," she said, her voice bitter. "But, yes, I suppose they felt sending me away was for the best."

Taking a deep breath, she wiped impatiently at her eyes. "But that's old news," she said. "Why am I in danger?"

Mary pushed the yearbook across the table to her, the book open to the page of the girls in front of the stadium. "This photo is what has us concerned," Mary said. "All of the girls in this photo are dead. Except for you and Katie Mahoney."

Faith looked at the photo and then up at Mary. "All of them are dead?" she asked. "How?"

"They all committed suicide," Ian said. "According to the police reports."

"Why would they do that?" she asked.

"That's the mystery," Mary replied. "None of them had reason or showed signs they were contemplating suicide. We're concerned that perhaps it isn't what it seems."

Faith shook her head. "I don't understand. It's not what it seems?"

"They might have been killed, but made to look like it was suicide," Ian said.

"And they all died on the anniversary of Hope's death," Mary added.

"Which is only two days away," Faith said. "What should I do?"

Ian reached over and closed the book. "Who might think they needed to avenge Hope's death?" he asked.

"The only person I can think of is Nick," she said. "He thought he was in love with Hope."

"Thought he was in love?" Mary asked.

"On the day Hope died she saw him kissing me," she said. "It seems his loyalties weren't what she thought."

"If he wasn't in love with her, why would he kill the others?" Mary asked.

"Guilt," Faith suggested. "Maybe he felt that his betrayal caused her to kill herself and he can't accept the guilt, so he blames others."

"Do you feel guilty about Hope's death?" Ian asked.

Staring down at the table, she was quiet for a few moments. Finally, she looked up and met Ian's eyes. "When my sister died, I died too," she said. "We were twins. No matter how much we disagreed with each other, we had that bond. It's hard for one to go on without the other. I can't tell you how many times I wished it had been me who died."

"I'm so sorry," Ian said. "I can't imagine."

"Most people can't," she agreed. "But I won't let her legacy die and I want to be sure something like this doesn't happen to other young girls."

"For the next few days we want you to be very careful," Mary said. "If you'd like, we can arrange police protection."

Shaking her head, she turned to Mary. "No, I don't think I could stand having someone watch me, especially this week," she said. "I really need my privacy this week. But I promise, I'll watch my back and if I feel nervous in any way, I'll call the police."

"We just warned Katie that she should not eat or drink anything that she hasn't prepared herself or was able to see prepared," Ian said. "We'd offer you the same advice."

"Katie? Katie Mahoney is still in town?" she asked.

"Aye, she's Katie Brennan now," Ian replied. "She has a wonderful family."

"That's great," Faith said. "I'd like to see her sometime. Maybe after all of this is over."

"I'm sure she'd like that," Ian said. "Once you're both safe and sound."

"Could you tell her something for me?" Faith asked, looking at Mary.

"Of course," Mary agreed.

"Tell her I'm sorry this has happened. I always considered her such a good friend and she shouldn't have to deal with this."

"I'll tell her," Mary said. "And I'm sure she'll be grateful."

Chapter Thirty-six

"That was a fairly odd conversation," Mary said, as they drove away from the law offices.

"Odd? In what way?" Ian asked.

"I don't quite know," she replied. "There's just something wrong here. My gut tells me there's something right in front of our faces, but I can't put a finger on it yet."

"Ah, well, then, your gut," he said. "Perhaps it was the brat and sauerkraut you had for lunch between Katie's house and seeing Faith. That would set my gut to having a funny feeling."

"Obviously you haven't spent years as a Chicago cop," she replied. "That was a gourmet lunch."

"You've got a stomach of iron, Mary O'Reilly," he said, shaking his head.

"Oh, and this from the man who enjoys a wee haggis sandwich," she replied.

"And what's wrong with a wee bit of haggis?" he asked. "At least it's not smothered in pickled cabbage."

"Don't knock it until you've tried it," she said.

"How do you say it…? Same goes," he replied.

She giggled. "Somehow it doesn't sound the same coming from you."

"Well, um, get over yourself," he teased, trying to use an American accent and failing.

Laughing, she turned the car onto the highway. "We're definitely going to have to work on that, Ian."

He turned and looked out the window. "And where, might I ask, are we going?"

Mary smiled and wiggled her eyebrows. "Back to the scene of the crime, of course."

The drive back to the house only took a few minutes. After they parked, Mary walked around to the back of her car and opened the trunk. Inside were a folding chair and a large heavy duty extension cord.

Ian looked over her shoulder. "Are we reenacting the crime?" he asked.

"Got it in one," she replied. "I thought if we reenacted it, we might be able to figure out what those thumps we heard on the recording were."

She pulled the spare key out of her purse and opened the door.

The house was quiet and the fog still hadn't completely cleared, which didn't encourage much natural light through the windows. Ian carried the chair and Mary carried the cord up the stairs to the bedroom. The room was empty, as it had been during their previous visit, but there was a subtle difference in the atmosphere this time.

"Something's changed," Mary whispered to Ian.

"Aye, there's a shadow in the room today," he agreed. "I feel someone's watching us."

The hairs began to tingle on the back of her neck and she forced herself not to turn around. "You're right," she said. "She's close."

Mary carried the cord to the closet, tied the end to the closet doorknob and unwrapped the rest as she walked to the middle of the room. Ian had set the folding chair underneath the fan and was ready to step up on it when Mary met him with the cord. "I'll tie it up," he said.

Pausing, Mary shook her head. "I have a feeling I need to do this," she said. "If we're trying to reenact it, a woman should be setting things up."

"Well, then, I'll hold the chair," Ian said. "Because I don't think it's as sturdy as the original one was."

"I'd really appreciate that," Mary said, stepping up on the chair and feeling it wobble slightly beneath her.

She looped the cord and tossed it over the vertical bar of the ceiling fan. It flew over and slipped down through the blades. Mary caught both ends and pulled them tight. She looked at the cord and the fan and shook her head. "I don't think once around would have done it," she said. "I think it would have at least been doubled."

"Aye, she would have wanted it to be secure," Ian agreed.

Mary tossed it up again and pulled it tight. "Now it's ready," she said.

She pulled the end taut, letting any extra cord slip over the fan and through her fingers. Then she picked up the extra length and created a noose that hung at her head level. Tugging on it, she tested it for strength. "This will do the trick," she said.

Suddenly the temperature of the room dropped and the shadows grew darker. "Ian," Mary said, looking down at him. "Are you feeling...?"

The bedroom door slammed shut, the force shaking the room, stopping Mary mid-sentence. Then she heard a soft creak above her. She looked up to see the ceiling fan starting to turn on its own. Slowly, the noose began to rise as the cord twisted through the blades and wrapped around the bar. It swung upward above the chair in a macabre dance.

Mary turned to look down at Ian and found herself, instead, staring into the face of the ghost, dangling by an unseen noose. Mary gasped as she looked at the girl; her face was blue, her lips purple, her head angled to one side and her eyes closed in death. Suddenly her eyelids burst open and she stared at Mary with anger and loathing. "No!" she screamed. "Go away!"

The chair wobbled as Mary jumped and she felt herself falling backward. Strong arms caught her around her waist and lowered her safely to the ground.

Shaken, her voice trembled as she stammered, "Thank you. I didn't expect..."

"Aye, that was a closer encounter than usual."

197

She looked up, but the ghost was gone and her knees felt shaky. "I think I'm going to sit down," she whispered, as she lowered herself to the chair.

"Sounds like a good idea," Ian replied, sitting down on the floor next to her. "Have you ever had an experience like this?"

Mary took a shaky breath. "No, not that I can remember. And I can assure you, I would have remembered."

"She was angry. She was almost violent."

"Was she trying to stop you from killing yourself?" he asked. "Did she think you were going to use the noose?"

Pausing for a moment, she looked up at the cord flapping against the blades of the fan. "Well, I suppose she might have thought…

"I wasn't trying to kill myself," she said aloud. "I was just trying to see what happened to you."

The door slammed again and they both jumped. "Okay, this is really getting on my nerves now," Ian said.

"Look at the ceiling fan," Mary said, pointing up to the fan that was now slowing.

"It's turning off," he replied, standing up. "What the…?"

He walked over to the door, opened it and slammed it again. The whir of the ceiling fan's motor could be heard again as the blades gained momentum. Reaching over, he turned off the wall switch and the fan slowed again.

"There's a short in the system," he said. "This wasn't a suicide, it was an accident. The noise we heard, someone walked out of here, slammed the door and turned on the fan."

The ghost appeared in front of Mary. Her neck was bruised where the cord had cut her, her face was still positioned in an unnatural angle and her blue face was swollen. "Save my sister," she gasped, as if her throat was still compressed. "Please, save my sister."

Then she faded away.

Chapter Thirty-seven

Mary slipped on her robe and tied the belt tightly around her waist. She glanced at the radio-alarm clock on the dresser and the green glowing numbers told her it was twelve-thirty. She had been trying to sleep for the past two hours, but the vision of Hope Foley's ghost kept going through her mind. It wasn't exactly that the vision was disturbing, although it was, because Mary had seen a number of disturbing things before. There was just something about the whole situation that bothered her and she just couldn't put her finger on it.

She opened the door to her room and padded down the hall. Placing her hand on the doorknob of Clarissa's room, she slowly turned it, opening the door quietly so she could peek in without disturbing the little girl's sleep. The room was dark, except for the soft glow of the nightlight that shone at the head of the bed. Mary could see Clarissa sleeping soundly, snuggled into her pillow, a soft snore coming from her open mouth. She came closer to pull up the blanket that had been kicked off, when she saw them and stopped.

Becca and Henry stood at the foot of the bed looking down on their sleeping child. They glanced up and smiled at Mary. "She looks good," Henry said. "You folks are doing a good job."

"Thank you," Mary whispered, watching to be sure she didn't disturb Clarissa. "She was already a secure and loving child. She couldn't have had better parents."

"We loved her," Becca said, "with all our hearts."

"She told me," Mary replied. "She always knew she was loved."

Becca looked back down on Clarissa, a wistful look on her face. "My funeral is tomorrow," Becca said. "Will she be okay?"

"She'll have lots of support," Mary said. "But it will still be hard on her, I'm sure. It's hard to lose the people you love most in the world."

The young mother turned and met Mary's eyes. "She's coming to love you. I heard her ask you if you would be her mother," Becca said. "Thank you for that."

"It's hard not to love her," Mary replied, turning and looking at the sleeping child. "And I will be sure she remembers that she was lucky enough to have three mothers."

"We're not sure if we'll be back after tonight," Henry said. "Now that we know she's safe..."

His voice broke; Becca wrapped her arm around Henry and hugged him. "And now that she's settling in," she continued, "we can move on."

"But we can... We get to watch," Henry said, his voice tight with emotion. "We get to watch her grow up."

"It's nice to know you'll be watching," Mary said, her eyes filling with tears. "She always believed that you would be."

Becca's gaze turned back to her sleeping daughter. Henry slipped his arm from her hold and placed it over her shoulders, hugging her to him.

Suddenly Mary felt like she was intruding on a very private moment. There was nothing she could say or do to make their final moments with their child any easier. "I'm going to leave you two to be alone with her," she said. "I'll be sure she never forgets you."

"Thank you," they said, their gazes not straying from the bed.

Mary quietly slipped out of the room and closed the door. She met Mike in the hallway, who motioned for her to follow him and, silently, they both went downstairs to the kitchen.

"How are you holding up?" he asked gently.

She busied herself by filling the kettle with water and placing it on the stove. She was feeling a little overwhelmed and somewhat guilty. Bradley had his daughter. He was finally reunited with her. They were all going to be a family. They were going to be happy. But Becca and Henry had to move on without her.

"Mary, love doesn't die," Mike said.

She froze in the middle of taking a cup out of the cupboard. "Are you reading minds now?" she asked.

He smiled at her. "It doesn't take a mind-reader to understand what you're feeling," he said. "Becca and Henry aren't losing her. They're just relocating for the time being."

"But what about all of those things they're going to miss?" she argued. "Her first date. Prom. Graduation. Marriage. Her first child."

"You and Bradley will be there for her," he said. "And all of those siblings you're going to provide."

"All of those siblings?" Mary asked.

Mike nodded and leaned back against the doorway. "Oh, yeah, God told me you were going to have at least eight kids," he said.

"What?" she asked, panic whipping through her body.

"See, now you don't feel so guilty," he replied with a grin. "It worked."

"Mike," she began.

"Mary, just listen for a moment," he interrupted. "Henry wasn't lying. He and Becca get to watch her grow up. They will be able to experience all of those joys you and Bradley are going to share with her. And, time in heaven, it's a little different than time here on earth. What takes so long down here is only a moment in heaven. They won't be parted from her for very long from their perspective."

Sighing, she took the cup down and placed it on the counter. "Really?"

He came over and stood next to her. "Really," he said. "And what more could any parents want than one of God's special warriors to help raise their daughter?"

"Who?"

Rolling his eyes, he sighed, "You, Mary O'Reilly. You."

The kettle started to whistle and Mary reached over, turned the stove off and moved the kettle to another burner. "Thanks Mike. Are you sure you aren't my guardian angel?" she asked.

"Now how could that have worked, when you've been my guardian angel ever since I met you?"

She smiled and then yawned. "Oh, I'm so sorry."

Mike took the cup and placed it back in the cupboard. "Go to bed, Mary," he ordered tenderly.

She nodded obediently and started back up the stairs. He watched her go and then softly added, "And try to let the world take care of itself for a little while."

Chapter Thirty-eight

A small group of mourners gathered in the chapel at the mortuary the next morning. Clarissa stood near the casket, dressed in a gray smocked dress, black tights and patent leather shoes. She had one hand on the edge of the casket that held her mother and the other tightly gripping Bradley's hand. For the past hour she had greeted each visitor and thanked them politely for coming to her mother's funeral. She had smiled and answered questions and handled herself like a little adult.

Mary, Ian and Mike stood close by to offer their support. "She's handling this well," Mike said.

"Too well," Mary replied softly. "She's bottled everything up inside."

"Poor wee bairn," Ian said. "No child should have to go through this."

"How long has she been up there like that?" Margaret O'Reilly, Mary's mother, asked as she came up behind Mary.

"Ma, you came," Mary said, giving her a hug.

"Well of course we came," she replied. "The child's going to be my granddaughter. You think we wouldn't be here?"

"We?" Mary asked.

"Your da is outside parking the car," she said. "Sean, Art and Tommy will be arriving soon."

"Thank you," Mary said, her heart full.

Her mother kissed her on the cheek. "Now, introduce me to my granddaughter."

They walked over to Clarissa and Bradley. "Margaret, you came," Bradley said.

"We're family," she said, kissing Bradley on the cheek, and then she bent down and offered her hand to Clarissa. "How do you do, young lady?"

Clarissa looked up and smiled politely. "I'm fine, thank you," she replied.

"Well, now, I don't see how you can be fine on a day such as today," Margaret said. "But I admire you for saying so."

"Thank you," Clarissa replied, wrinkling her nose in confusion. "What do you mean?"

"I mean, it's a hard day for you," she said. "And you've been through a lot during your young life. And if you wanted to not be fine. And if you wanted to cry a little. That would be perfectly fine."

"But I'm supposed to be a brave soldier," Clarissa replied. "That's what my mommy told me when my daddy died."

"Ah, and your mother was a wise woman," Margaret said. "Because she knew you would have to be strong to deal with the next months. But now, you've a new father and mother, who can be strong for you. So, you can be sad if you'd like."

Clarissa looked up at Bradley. "Can I?" she asked.

He squatted down next to her and gently pushed her hair away from her eyes. "Yes, you can," he said. "It's okay not to be strong today."

"In Ireland, where I come from, when someone dies we tell stories about them," Margaret said. "We laugh and we cry and then we laugh some more. We celebrate their life."

Clarissa studied Margaret for a moment. "Who are you?" she finally asked.

Chuckling, Margaret gave Clarissa a quick hug. "Well, I'm your grandmother," she said. "And that big man who's coming our way is your grandfather. We're Mary's ma and da."

"I have a grandmother and a grandfather now?" she asked, her voice filled with awe.

"Yes," Margaret said. "And you have three uncles. They're good for spoiling you."

Margaret turned to Bradley. "Would it be proper for me to take this young lady to the side, so she can tell me a little about her lovely mother?" she asked.

"Sure. Yes. I suppose that would be fine," he said, confused by her request.

Mary stood next to him and they watched Margaret and Timothy lead Clarissa to a small private area.

"Why did she want to do that?" Bradley asked Mary.

"Because she understands that in order to begin to grieve, you have to allow yourself to feel. You can't always be brave, because then you just bottle up all the emotions," she explained. "You have to give yourself permission to be sad."

"She never got to be sad for Henry," he said. "She never got to grieve."

"Well, now, perhaps she can grieve for both of them," Mary said.

She looked across the room and saw Clarissa sobbing inside Margaret's embrace.

"It's hard to see her crying," Bradley said.

"But crying is the best thing for her," Mary replied. "All of that emotion that's bottled up inside can come out. Then the healing can begin."

Bradley nodded. "I remember," he said slowly. "Mike did that for me. He made me stop at the cemetery in Sycamore after I'd met with Jeannine's parents. He made me talk about her and then I just started to cry. And once the tears started, I couldn't stop them."

"How did you feel?" she asked.

"Like a burden had been taken off my chest, like I didn't always have to be strong," he said and then he sighed deeply. "I have a lot to learn about being a good father."

She turned to him and placed a gentle kiss on his lips. "You're doing a fine job."

Chapter Thirty-nine

Katie, Clifford and Maggie arrived at the funeral home about twenty minutes later. Katie hurried over to Mary and Bradley as soon as she walked in the door. "I am so sorry we are late," she said. "Clifford insisted on coming and he was delayed at work. How are things going?"

"Things are fine, Katie," Bradley said. "Thanks for coming."

"How's Clarissa doing?" she asked.

Mary looked across the room to where Clarissa still sat with her parents, now chatting happily with them. "I think she's doing fine," Mary said. "And I think having Maggie here is going to do her a world of good."

Maggie looked around the room and saw Clarissa. She hurried over to her, excited that this was her very first funeral. She hadn't been allowed to come when Clarissa's daddy had died. "Clarissa, I'm here," she said, as she approached her.

"Maggie, guess what," Clarissa said, slipping off the chair she'd been sitting on. "I have lots of grandparents now. These ones are from Mary."

"Grandparents are great," Maggie said. "They let you get away with all kinds of stuff."

Margaret chuckled. "We've heard about you, Maggie," she said. "It sounds like you've been a great friend to Clarissa."

"We're best friends," Maggie informed her.

"Well, that's the best kind," Margaret said.

"Do you want to see my mommy?" Clarissa asked.

"Is it okay to look at her?" Maggie asked. "'Cause she's dead."

"Uh huh, everyone does it. It's so you can say goodbye to her."

"Okay," Maggie said hesitantly. "I guess."

Clarissa led Maggie across the room to Becca's casket and the two little girls peered at the woman lying inside. "It kind of looks like your mom, but kinda not," Maggie said.

"That's 'cause it's not really my mom anymore," Clarissa explained.

"Why not?"

Clarissa turned to Maggie. "My grandma told me that our bodies are like gloves and our spirits are like hands," Clarissa explained. "When we're born, our bodies slip over our spirits, just like gloves slip over hands. And they move when we move and talk when we talk, just like gloves move when our hands move. Then, when we die, we leave our bodies here on earth, like taking off a glove. And our spirits get to go live with God."

"That's why your mommy looks like that," Maggie said. "'Cause the most important part of her went to live with God."

Clarissa nodded her head. "Uh-huh."

"But don't you miss her?"

"I miss her lots," Clarissa said. "And it's okay to be sad and miss her. But she and Daddy Henry are in heaven watching over me."

Mary came over and joined the girls. "How are you two doing?" she asked.

"Clarissa's mommy and daddy are watching her from heaven now," Maggie said.

Mary pictured the two standing over their daughter's bed last night. "Yes, they are," she agreed. "And they will always be watching over her."

Steve Turner, the funeral director, crossed the room and spoke with Bradley and then came over to where Mary and the girls stood. "It's time for the service," he said. "Are you ready?"

Clarissa nodded and they all moved forward to take their seats at the front of the chapel. Mary looked around the room and saw Ian stop and speak with Katie. She was relieved he was keeping an eye on her. But her curiosity was peaked when she watched them leave the room together.

"Katie I wonder if I can speak with you for a moment?" Ian asked.

"Sure, Ian, what do you need?" she replied.

"I'm wondering what you know about hypnotism," he said. "Have you ever been hypnotized before?"

Chapter Forty

An hour later, Clarissa sat between Bradley and Mary in the main funeral car, following the hearse, as they headed to the cemetery. "How are you doing, sweetheart?" Bradley asked.

"I'm doing better," she said. "I'm still sad, but it doesn't hurt as much."

"I know just what you mean," he replied. "We're going to have your mommy, Becca, buried next to your daddy."

"But, really, they're in heaven, right?"

"Exactly," Mary said. "This is just the place where we put the gloves."

"Exactly," Clarissa repeated.

"The gloves?" Bradley asked.

Mary smiled at Clarissa and winked. "We'll tell you all about it later," she said.

The service at the graveside was short and soon Mary and Katie were following Clarissa and Maggie across the lawn to get back in the cars. Mary was eager to find out what Ian and Katie had been discussing.

"Katie, I was wondering…" Mary began.

"Ms. O'Reilly. Ms. O'Reilly," Nick came rushing across the grounds toward them. "I really need to speak with you."

"Nick? Nick Kazakos?" Katie asked. "I haven't seen you for years."

"Katie Mahoney?" Nick asked.

Katie nodded. "Well, I'm Katie Brennan now. How are you doing?"

"As well as can be expected when you live your life without the person who was supposed to be your soul mate," he snapped back at her.

"Oh," she said, confused by his anger. "I'm so sorry."

"Yeah, well it's nice that one of us can live happily ever after," he said.

"I'm sorry," Katie repeated. "I don't know what to say."

"Well, maybe you should have said something twenty years ago when Hope was looking for a friend," he retorted. "Maybe if she'd had a friend, she wouldn't have killed herself."

Katie took a deep breath and shook her head. "If I had any idea," she began. "If I could have done anything…"

"Yeah, easy to say now," he interrupted.

Katie stepped back as if she'd been slapped. "I'd better go," she said. "Mary, I'll meet you at the cars."

Katie hurried away, following after the girls.

"That was not only rude, but it was stupid," Mary said. "Katie would have been Hope's friend if Hope had let her. Hope assumed Katie was Faith's friend and so she didn't speak to Katie."

"I don't believe that," he said. "And I don't believe you."

"What good would come from me lying to you?" Mary asked.

"Well, maybe you're trying to save your friend's life," he said.

Mary caught him by the collar of his shirt and pushed him up against the nearest tree. "Are you telling me that you killed those other women?" she asked.

His eyes grew wide and his voice shook. "No, no, I didn't mean that at all."

"What did you mean?" she asked.

"I only meant that if people thought she wasn't Faith's friend, whoever was killing her friends wouldn't kill Katie. That's all."

Mary loosened her hold. "I'm watching you, Nick," she said. "Nothing had better happen to my friend or I'll come looking for you."

"You can't do that," he insisted. "You can't threaten me like that."

"Oh, I can't?" she asked. "What are you going to do about it?"

"I'll call the…" He stopped as he watched Bradley hurry toward them.

"Mary, is everything okay here?" he asked.

"Nick, I'd like you to meet my fiancé, Chief of Police Bradley Alden," she said pointedly. "You do understand my message now, don't you?"

Nick nodded.

"Good, have a nice day, Nick," Mary said, and then she slipped her arm around Bradley's and let him escort her to the car.

"What was that all about?" he asked.

"Basic intimidation practice," she said. "He's on the short list of the people who could've been killing off Faith Foley's friends and I just wanted to let him know that Katie Brennan was off limits."

Bradley stopped walking and looked back over his shoulder. "You think he killed those women?" he asked.

"Well, I don't have any evidence," she admitted. "I just didn't want him to think that taking out Katie was going to be easy."

"And what was the message you sent him?"

"I told him that if anything were to happen to Katie, I'd come looking for him," she replied. "And then he told me that he'd call the police."

Bradley chuckled softly. "And that's when I walked in."

She squeezed his arm. "Your timing was impeccable."

"Yeah, but remember, I don't know anything about this," he said.

"About what?" she asked with a smile.

"Exactly."

Chapter Forty-one

Nick watched them walk away, his anger building. He could tell they were laughing at him. *Just who is she to tell me what to do? She's nobody! She's less than nobody! I'll show her. But what can I do?*

"I don't believe you," he whispered. "I don't believe you at all."

He stormed back to the small apartment he kept over the maintenance garage. The room was sparsely furnished, mostly with odds and ends he picked up at garage sales or discarded pieces of furniture left by the curb for the garbage collectors. The only thing he spent his money on was his computer system. His apartment had the fastest internet connection and he had been able to master the art of hacking in his spare time.

"I'll find out who you really are," he said, as he entered information into his search engine, punching the keys of his keyboard angrily.

"Mary O'Reilly," he whispered, "what do you really do?"

An hour later, Nick pushed himself away from his computer and walked to the window that overlooked the cemetery. He had never believed in ghosts. Never really thought much about what happened to someone once they died.

He looked over the grounds surrounding him. The tombstones and monuments cast long shadows in the late afternoon sun and the fog was starting to develop once again. Were their ghosts down there? Spirits who were restless because they still had unfinished business?

He jumped as a bird flew past his window.

He had never before been spooked in his apartment – until now.

He turned on a few more lights and grabbed a bag of chips from the pantry. Then he sat back in front of his computer and reread the newspaper articles about Mary O'Reilly. She was no researcher. According to the information he'd read, she solved murder cases. Why would she be interested in Hope? Hope wasn't murdered, she committed...

His thought process froze.

Everyone thought Hope had killed herself. What if she hadn't? What if she'd been murdered?

That really made much more sense. She would have left him a note.

He sat back in his chair and thought back to the night she died. He'd followed her home, tried to get her to talk to him, but she'd refused. He'd even gone to the door, but her mother had shooed him away. But he couldn't leave, not after Hope had seen what he'd done. He corrected himself, what Faith made him do. He would have never been unfaithful to Hope if Faith hadn't seduced him.

He leaned forward once again and found the link he'd been looking for. A couple of years ago he'd hacked into the coroner's computer system because there was some missing information on a death certificate and he hadn't reviewed the paperwork until the night before the funeral. Now, he cruised the data, picking up tidbits of information about the deceased members of the community the papers left out.

He searched the system and finally found the report. Scanning the form he hurried down to the comments section. *Subject was a Caucasian woman, sixteen years of age. Cause of death: asphyxiation from hanging. Subject was found by her mother hanging from a heavy duty electric cord...*

An electric cord? A vision suddenly flashed into his mind. Faith had come out of the house and walked over to the gardening shed. He nearly came out of his hiding place, thinking it was Hope. But he realized quickly that it was Faith. He could always tell them apart, even when they were little and looked much more similar. Faith went into the shed and came out with an extension cord.

He hadn't thought anything of it at the time. He'd always assumed Hope had used a rope. But Faith got a cord! Faith carried it into the house! Faith murdered Hope!

He stood up and started to pace around the room. What could he do? Who would believe him now? It had been twenty years and Faith, well, Faith was a Foley. No one would believe him.

He didn't care if anyone believed him. He needed to avenge Hope.

Chapter Forty-two

Mary, Bradley and Ian sat at the kitchen table with a whiteboard in front of them. They had outlined the timeline of Hope's death and the other victims. They also listed all of the pertinent facts they had found in the police reports.

Mary sat back in her chair, took a bite of a gingersnap and shook her head. "I know I'm missing something," she said. "But I can't see it. Not yet."

"It'll come to you," Ian said. "You have to stop thinking about it."

Bradley got up, walked into the kitchen and pulled another Diet Pepsi out. "I have one question for both of you," he said. "Why? Why would Hope pretend to commit suicide? If the whole thing was a deception gone wrong, what was her point?"

He brought his soda back to the table and sat down next to them.

"Most teens who have tried to commit suicide say they felt they were trying to escape from a situation that seemed impossible to deal with," Mary said. "They don't really want to die, but at that moment, they don't see that they have other choices."

"There are always choices," Ian said.

"Sure, that's easy for you to say," Mary replied. "But when you're in the midst of it, the future can look pretty terrifying. They're not thinking of their choices or what they'd be missing."

"Aye, and there's the point," Ian said. "Instead of playing through and seeing the outcome, we're trying to cheat the game. All we end up doing is cheating ourselves and our families."

"You sound like this is hitting pretty close to home, Ian," Mary said. "Are you okay?"

He sighed and finally turned and faced both of them.

"My father died when I was thirteen," Ian said. "It was an accident, a horrible accident, and my mother took it very hard. She didn't talk to me... She didn't talk to anyone; she would just sit in his study and cry. I lost both my father and my mother. I was alone with my grief and I really didn't know how to handle it. One afternoon I decided that it would be better to be with my father than my mother, and I grabbed my hunting rifle and went on a walk on the estate."

"Oh, Ian," Mary cried.

He sat back against his chair and put his hands behind his head. "I can remember the day like it was yesterday," he recalled. "The sun was shining, reflecting in the brook that runs through the woods. The birds were singing. The sky was bright blue. And I was determined to die. I walked to the spot my father and I used when we would hunt. It was a quiet glen, hidden away and peaceful. I got out the gun, loaded it and sat down on a large log."

"And then my father came striding out of the woods behind me," he said with a sad smile. "He asked me what in blue blazes I thought I was doing and I told him, through my tears, that I wanted to be with him. I didn't want to be alone any longer. I couldn't take the pain."

He took a deep breath. "My father sat down on the log next to me, as he'd done hundreds of times, except this time he was a ghost. He asked me if I knew what it felt like to die and, of course, I said no."

Ian stopped and chuckled. "I can remember his words so clearly," he said, lowering his voice a bit deeper and thickening his accent a bit. "Then why in the world would you give up something you know and take a chance with the unknown? What if you don't like it? What if it's worse? What have you then? A big waste of your life, that's what you have."

"But I'd have none of it," Ian said. "But I'm so unhappy, I told him. Mother doesn't love me anymore because she misses you. The lads at school think I'm daft because I can see ghosts. I really don't fit in here in this world."

"What did your father say to that?" Bradley asked.

"He put his arm around me. It was a strange feeling, like electricity, but milder. He asked me about the ghosts I'd seen and if all of them were happy and satisfied. I shook my head and told him that no, they were mostly sad and had issues. Then he cuffed me gently on my head and asked me why in the world I thought my problems would go away in death, if the ghosts I dealt with still had all of their problems."

"I guess he had you there," Mary said. "I'd never thought of that."

"I put the rifle down and turned to him," he continued. "Then what am I supposed to do? I asked him. And he told me that I was supposed to be brave, but know there were going to be times when I felt afraid. I was supposed to love, but know there were times when my heart was going to be broken. I was supposed to look to the future, but know there were times when I would need to reflect upon the past. And when things get too hard to bear, I was just supposed to take tiny steps and look for the little daily miracles that showed me God cares about me and loves me."

Mary wiped a tear from her eye. "That was profound."

Ian smiled. "Aye, he had a way with words," he said. "So, I unloaded the rifle and walked home, with the sun on my back, the birds singing and the sky as blue as a robin's egg. And when I got home, I was greeted by the local constabulary. It seems my mother had gone into my father's study and loaded his hunting rifle and taken her own life."

"Oh, Ian, how could you go on after that?" Mary asked.

"I really didn't think I could," he said. "It was like this was a great joke God was playing on me. But I thought about what my father had said and I took tiny, really tiny, steps for a while. Getting out of bed was sometimes all I could accomplish in a day. But it was a step. I didn't look too far into the future, because I couldn't handle it yet. And finally, I could look back on all my tiny steps and realized I had moved forward. I had survived and I could begin to see the little miracles."

"I don't know if I could have been as strong as you were," Bradley said. "Especially when it seemed that God had forgotten you."

"Ah, and there's the irony of it. I finally recognized that the very first little miracle God sent me was that very day my mother took her life," he said. "Because I was out in the woods, speaking with my father, I wasn't home when she died. I didn't have to find her or see what happened. I was able to remember her as she had been."

"Do you really get little miracles every day?" Bradley asked.

Ian smiled and nodded. "Oh, aye, you just have to remember to look for them," he said. "They're often little things, but they're there."

Suddenly Mary sat up straight in her chair. "The little things," she repeated. "Ian, you're exactly right."

She grabbed the whiteboard and jotted down a list of facts they had gathered over the past few days.

"What is it?" Ian asked.

"I want to work it through in my mind for a bit longer, but Bradley, can you run a background check on Faith Foley for us?" she asked. "I want to know where she went after Hope's death, what her grades were like and anything else you can find."

"I'll do it first thing in the morning," Bradley said.

"And Ian, you and I are going back to the nursing home in the morning," Mary said. "I have a feeling that Gloria didn't tell us all she knew."

"Okay, you get to be Sherlock this time," Ian said with a wink.

"The game's afoot!" Mary replied.

Chapter Forty-three

The old pickup rattled down the street lined with expensive condos whose yards backed into the golf course and the park. Anyone that took the time to look at it would assume a delivery was being made. But most of the residents were too busy inside their homes on the cool spring evening to even take note of it. Nick parked a few doors away from Faith's condo, out of the glow of a streetlight and walked up the rain-slicked sidewalk.

Knocking on the door, he tapped his foot impatiently while he waited for her to answer it. He had pictured this meeting many times in his mind. In earlier versions, Faith would tell him that she wanted him and had always been jealous of Hope. She would throw her arms around him and beg him to take her. But this afternoon's rendition had a different twist. Faith had been begging him not to go to the authorities. Begging him not to tell anyone about the cord. She had dropped to her knees, pleading, telling him that she would do anything, anything if he would just keep her out of jail. And then the daydream got even more interesting.

The click of a deadbolt being pulled back snapped Nick back from his fantasy into reality. The door opened and Faith was standing in front of him, even more desirable than he had remembered. He took a deep breath, reminding himself that he had the upper hand. Remembering the lines he used in his daydream.

"It's been a long time, Faith," he said.

In his fantasy his voice had been deep and smooth, but somehow it came out breathless and squeaky.

"I'm sorry, do I know you?" Faith asked.

Nick was nonplussed for a moment. That wasn't the right line.

"Don't play games with me," he said. "I know you know who I am."

She shook her head. "Sorry, no."

"I'm Nick, dammit, Nick Kazakos."

She stared at him for a little bit longer. "From?"

"From high school," he said. "We were together in high school. I liked your sister, Hope, and you tried to seduce me."

"Really? I tried to seduce you?" she asked, with a quick laugh. "Was I drunk?"

This was not at all the way he had imagined it.

"Listen, I saw you with the cord that night your sister died," he blurted out. "I saw you take the extension cord from the gardener's shed and bring it back to the house."

Faith leaned against the doorjamb and smiled. "Well, why didn't you say something twenty years ago?" she asked.

"Because I thought Hope's death was a suicide," he said, his voice becoming frantic. "But I know the truth now."

She calmly folded her arms over her chest. "Do you?" she asked. "The truth? And what would the truth be?"

"You killed Hope," he stammered, spittle collecting on the corners of his mouth. "You did it. They covered it up, your parents. But you did it."

She smiled at him. "Why don't you come in Nick," she suggested, moving away from the door and motioning him into the room. "It seems we have a lot to discuss."

Chapter Forty-four

Mary opened the door to Clarissa's room and looked around in the dim morning light. Mike was sitting in the corner of the room, in an easy chair, and Clarissa was sound asleep in her bed, her blankets askew and her pillow on the floor.

"Rough night?" Mary asked Mike as she picked up the pillow and placed it on the end of the bed.

"Yeah, she was a little restless, but no nightmares," he said. "I think being with your mom did her a world of good."

"I agree, I'm so glad they all came yesterday," she said. "I think my brothers wore her out."

Nodding, Mike got up and stood next to Mary; both of them looked down at the sleeping child. "They made her laugh," he said. "She needed to be silly. She hasn't had nearly enough silly in her life."

Mary glanced around the room. "Did Henry or Becca...?"

Mike shook his head, interrupting her. "No, they've really moved on," he said. "You're her mother now, Mary."

Mary took a deep breath. "It's a little overwhelming," she said. "What if I mess up?"

"Well, I can pretty much guarantee that you'll mess up, say things you regret later, be unreasonable occasionally and even be cranky," Mike said. "That's all part of being a human parent. But the most important ingredient in the mix is unconditional love. Once you have that, you're golden."

Mary ran her hand tenderly over Clarissa's forehead. "Okay, I guess I'm golden," she whispered.

"Mom?" Clarissa mumbled, her eyes still closed.

Mary looked up at Mike, unsure.

"It's for you," he said, stepping back away from the bed.

Hesitantly, Mary leaned over the bed and kissed Clarissa on her cheek. "Good morning, sweetheart," she said.

Clarissa opened her eyes, took a moment to focus and smiled. "Good morning, Mom."

"How are you feeling today?" Mary asked.

Stretching slowly, Clarissa seemed to be taking inventory. "I think I'm good," she said, thoughtfully.

"Good enough to go to school?" Mary asked.

Nodding, Clarissa sat up and pushed the covers away. "Yes, because today is gym and art," she said, "my two favorite classes."

"Well, then, I suppose you should go," Mary replied. "What would you like to wear?"

Nearly fifteen minutes later, once the wardrobe decisions had been made, Mary and Clarissa climbed down the stairs toward the kitchen.

"Something smells good," Clarissa said, lifting her nose into the air and taking a deep sniff.

"It smells like blueberry muffins," Mary said, "but that's impossible. Only…"

"What's impossible?" Stanley asked, coming to the bottom of the stairs. "That old folks like us could get up early enough to surprise a couple of sleepy heads with muffins?"

Mary gave Stanley a big hug. "Welcome home," she said.

"Yeah, well, I'd still be on our honeymoon iffen I had any say in the matter," he grumbled.

"Now Stanley," Rosie called from the kitchen. "You know you were just as excited to come home."

Rosie came out of the kitchen, wiping her hands on the towel tucked into her waistband and enveloped Mary in a hug. "We heard about your newest family member and couldn't wait to meet her."

Clarissa had stopped several steps above them, not quite sure what she should do. When Mary held her hand up to her, she eagerly took it and came down the last few steps.

"Clarissa, I want you to meet two of my dearest friends," Mary said. "This is Mr…"

"Poppa Stanley," Stanley interrupted. "That's what all my grandkids call me. You just call me Poppa Stanley."

"And I'm your Nanna Rosie," Rosie said, coming forward and hugging the little girl. "We are so happy to meet you. We already love you."

Clarissa looked over at Mary. "I have more grandparents?" she asked, her eyes wide in wonder.

"I suppose you do," she replied with a wide smile. "And you'll meet more of your grandparents next week."

"How do you feel about blueberry muffins for breakfast?" Rosie asked.

"I feel very good about them," Clarissa answered, taking Rosie's hand and allowing her to lead her to the kitchen table. "Are you a good cooker?"

"She's the best cooker in the world," Stanley said with an indulgent smile. Then he turned to Mary and whispered, "How are things here?"

"Well, Gary Copper escaped from custody and we've had a couple of visits," Mary replied. "He was even bold enough to walk up to Clarissa at school. So, we've increased police security and we're being cautious."

Then she smiled at him. "Which reminds me, I need to change the password on my door lock. It seems just anyone can let themselves in."

Stanley laughed. "Not just anyone," he said. "Poppa and Nanna Wagner."

"Am I smelling muffins?" Ian asked as he half-stumbled down the stairs.

"Is that foreigner still here?" Stanley asked loudly.

231

Ian grinned. "Is that old man who stole my best girl here?"

"She chose the better man," Stanley replied.

Coming into the living room, Ian gave Stanley a hug. "Aye, that she did," he said. "Welcome back. And how was your honeymoon?"

"I ain't gonna kiss and tell, young man," Stanley said. "Suffice it to say, I'm the luckiest man in the world."

"Oh, Stanley, just stop it," Rosie said from the kitchen.

Ian walked over to her and gave her a hug. "Darling, are you sure you made the right decision?" he asked, snatching a muffin from the plate she was carrying. "You can still run away with me."

"Ian, I'm sorry, but Stanley completely stole my heart," she replied. "I'm afraid I'll have to turn you down."

He took a bite of the muffin. "Rosie, my heart," he said, his mouth full. "Do you, perhaps, have a sister?"

She giggled. "Oh, Ian."

At that moment Bradley walked into the house. He smelled the warm muffins and felt the love in the room. Rosie was bent over Clarissa, offering her another muffin. Stanley and Mary were laughing at something Ian had said and Ian was teasing Stanley. This was his family. These were the people who were going to help him raise his daughter. This was the security and love he'd longed for all of his life.

Clarissa looked over at Mary. "Am I going to have a sister?" she asked.

There was silence in the room for a moment. Mary turned and saw Bradley standing near the door and her face flushed. He immediately remembered the vision of her in his dream, pregnant and glowing. The perfect Madonna. He walked over to Mary and took her in his arms, kissing her tenderly. "Maybe someday, Clarissa," he said, still looking into Mary's eyes. "Maybe someday you will have a sister and a brother too."

"Well, you two can make smoochie faces with each other," Stanley growled. "I'm getting some muffins afore they're cold."

Clarissa laughed. "Smoochie faces? That's funny, Poppa Stanley."

"Poppa Stanley?" Bradley asked, one eyebrow raised.

"We're just one big happy family," Mary replied with a smile.

Bradley leaned forward and placed a kiss on her forehead. "Yes. Yes we are."

Chapter Forty-five

An hour later, the house was much quieter. Bradley had driven Clarissa to school and Rosie and Stanley had gone home so Mary and Ian could get some work done.

Bradley had brought Faith Foley's background check with him that morning and now Mary and Ian were finally getting around to reading it.

"I know it all revolves around Faith," Mary said, pulling up a chair at the table. "I just can't quite put my finger on what."

"Well, this ought to help," Ian said, lifting the multi-paged report up and dividing it into two piles. "I'll take the front half and you take the back half."

They both began to study the report, carefully inching their way down each sheet, looking for pertinent information.

"This is odd," Ian remarked.

"What?" Mary asked.

"The boarding school in Switzerland," Ian said. "It's a grand school, but it was generally known as a place where, um, larger girls could go and become a more acceptable size."

"Well, that's odd because all of the photos of Faith show her to be extremely thin," Mary said. "Is there another reason she would be sent there?"

"Well, maybe to learn how to be sympathetic to girls who weren't the perfect size 2," Ian suggested. "And for a generally good liberal arts education."

"Okay, that could be the ultimate therapy," Mary said. "Go to a school with a bunch of girls like your sister and become friends. Perhaps make amends for the mean things you did to her by being nice to others."

Ian shrugged and looked back down at the report. "Could be," he murmured, his focus back on the page.

"Her grades were really good," he commented. "And this isn't an easy school."

"That's odd, because her GPA in Freeport was really bad," Mary said. "She wasn't the scholar in the family."

"Well, tragedy changes people," he said.

They continued to read. "She went to Stanford after Switzerland," Mary said. "She got a B.S. in Psychology and then got her Law Degree. Sounds like the good grades continued.

"Wait, did you say a B.S. in Psychology?" Ian asked.

Mary nodded. "Why?"

"Stanford's Psychology Department has done a tremendous amount of research on using hypnosis," he said. "I worked with some people from Stanford when I learned how to hypnotize subjects for my research. They really are top of their game."

235

"Hypnosis. Really?" Mary asked. "Could someone be hypnotized to kill themselves?"

"Depends on the subject and the suggestion that was given," Ian said. "It's generally easier to have someone follow a hypnotic suggestion if they are in sympathy with the request."

"If someone made you feel that you might have been responsible for another's death, would that be sympathetic enough?" Mary asked.

"Aye, that would work," Ian said. "So Faith is avenging her sister's death."

"You would think that's the case," Mary said. "But that doesn't make sense with what we saw. Hope's death was an accident, she was playing…"

Mary stopped for a moment, stared into space and then quickly turned to Ian. "Do you still have the police report about Hope's death?"

Ian nodded and rustled through the pile of folders, finally pulling out the correct one. He handed it to Mary. Quickly flipping it open, she scanned the report looking for the coroner's report.

"This is it," she said. "This is what's wrong with the whole thing."

"What?" Ian asked.

"The coroner lists Hope's weight at 116," Mary said. "From the photos we have of Hope, there was no way she was 116 pounds."

"Could be a typo," Ian said.

Mary nodded. "Yes, or it could be something entirely different. Let's go to the nursing home and find out."

Chapter Forty-six

True to her word, Katie Brennan planned on spending the entire day in her house working on projects. She had locked both the front and back door and was starting to clean out the hallway closet when there was a sharp rap on the front door.

"I'm not home," she muttered to herself, ignoring the knock and sorting through the stacks of magazines stored in boxes.

The knock repeated, more urgently this time.

"I'm not..." she paused.

What if one of the kids had been hurt and they hadn't been able to get a hold of her? What if the police were outside her door? What if the house next door was on fire?

She scrambled to her feet and hurried to the front door. Peering through the peephole, she saw Faith Foley standing on her porch.

"How odd," she thought aloud. "I haven't seen Faith in years."

She opened the door.

"Oh, Katie, I'm so sorry to bother you," Faith said quickly. "I've been speaking with your friends, Mary and Ian, and they told me about the suicides. I mean, I guess the murders."

Katie nodded. "Yes, it's pretty weird, isn't it?"

"Yes, it's weird and scary," Faith agreed. "And they said you and I were the only two left in the yearbook photo. I am so sorry I dragged you into this, I had no idea…"

"Well, of course you didn't," Katie said. "How could you even imagine that so many years later someone would be avenging Hope's death?"

Faith hung her head and pulled out a tissue. "It's just like it was yesterday," she said quietly into her tissue. "I can still remember her in such detail."

"Oh, Faith, I'm so sorry," Katie said. "I can't even imagine what it's like to lose someone you love so much."

Faith lifted her head and dabbed around her eyes. "It's just…" she began and then she took a shuddering breath. "Every year, on the anniversary of her death, I have a private memorial service for her. But this year, I hate to admit that I'm afraid to be alone."

"Well, I understand that," Katie said. "Mary said that whoever did this would be looking at either you or me."

Hesitating for just a moment, Faith lifted her head and smiled. "Exactly, we're the only people we can trust," she exclaimed. "That's why I'm here."

Confused, Katie shook her head. "Why?"

"Because I need you to come with me to the memorial service," she explained. "I can trust you and I really need to do this for Hope."

Stepping back, Katie hesitated. "I don't think that's a good idea," she said. "Mary was pretty adamant about me staying home."

"But if someone was actually looking for you, wouldn't they come to your home first?" Faith reasoned. "And if someone was looking for me, they'd come to my office or my house."

"Yes, that makes sense."

"So, we can go back to my old house," Faith said. "I still have a key. We could have a quick memorial service in Hope's bedroom. It would mean so much to me. Please, Katie, I can't take no for an answer."

"I don't know…" Katie stammered.

"Please, Katie, I don't want to be out there alone," she said.

Finally, Katie agreed. "Okay, just let me call Mary and tell her what we're doing."

"Why don't you get ready and I call Mary," Faith suggested. "Then we can get going faster."

"Okay," Katie said, opening the door and inviting Faith in. "Just have a seat in the living room and I'll be down in a few minutes."

Katie ran upstairs to change from sweats into jeans, a nicer blouse and shoes. She grabbed her cell phone and was about to stuff it in her purse, when she decided to send a quick text to Mary. *"Sorry, don't be mad. But Faith was pretty insistent. No one will think to look for us at her old house."*

She pressed "send" and started to place the phone in the pocket of her purse, but stopped, shook her head, and instead slipped it into the pocket of her jeans. Then she hurried downstairs.

"I'll drive," Faith said. "That way it will look like you're still home."

"Great idea," Katie agreed. "Let's go."

Chapter Forty-seven

Mary and Ian hurried down the hall of the nursing home and found Gloria Foley sitting in a chair, looking out the window once again. "Gloria, it's so good to see you again," Mary said with false brightness. "Ian and I just wanted to stop by and thank you for all of your help."

Gloria turned to Mary, her face showing her obvious confusion. "I'm sorry, have we met?" she asked.

"Why yes, we have," Mary said, sitting down across from her. "We spent some time with you earlier this week discussing your beautiful daughter."

Gloria smiled. "You knew Faith?" she asked.

Mary nodded. "Yes, I met her a couple of times. Do you miss her?"

Gloria nodded. "I can't believe she's gone," she said sadly. "Of course, I'm not supposed to speak about it. You know, it's a secret."

"I know," Mary said. "And I must say your family has done an admirable job of hiding things."

Gloria nodded and smiled brightly. "Well, of course, we knew no one would believe that Faith would kill herself," she explained. "She was too popular. Too well-loved."

"And if the police investigated, they would learn the truth," Mary said, encouraging Gloria.

"Yes," Gloria replied, "it was bad enough that she was dead, but to learn that she had been taunting her sister. Encouraging Hope to kill herself. Well, her name would have been ruined."

Ian pulled up a seat next to both of them. "So, Faith set up the noose and was standing on the chair when Hope came into the room," he said, nodding in understanding. "She laughed at Hope and told her she should just end it."

"Yes, and then Hope slammed out of the room and that stupid short in the electric panel caused the fan to start to spin," Gloria said, "causing the cord to tighten around Faith's neck."

"So it was just an accident," Mary said.

"Well, if Hope hadn't slammed out of the room, Faith would still be alive," Gloria said sternly. "I told her so that evening. Faith was just teasing her. She didn't need to go overboard like that."

"You told Hope that she killed her sister," Ian asked.

"Yes, I did," Gloria replied. "And I told her that no one would believe Faith had died, but everyone would believe Hope had died. So she would just have to change places with her sister."

"You sent her away?" Mary asked.

"Of course I did," she said brightly. "No one would look at Hope and think it was Faith. She needed to lose some of her fat and learn how to take care of herself."

"And she didn't argue with you?" Ian asked. "She didn't think it was unfair?"

Shaking her head, Gloria eyed Ian with confusion. "Well, no, of course not," she said. "What girl wouldn't want to have the opportunity to be Faith instead of Hope? I gave her the chance of a lifetime."

"Does she ever visit you?" Mary asked.

Gloria smiled. "Yes, once every four years she comes and visits. She always tells me that she's just done what Faith would want her to do on the anniversary of her death. Every four years, just like clockwork."

"And would this be the year for the visit?" Ian asked.

Nodding, Gloria pulled out a small card. "See, she sent me this earlier in the week," she said. "She will be visiting me later this afternoon."

Chapter Forty-eight

Faith pulled her car up to the front of the house and turned to Katie. "I really appreciate you doing this for me," she said. "This is going to be such a special memorial service with you here."

"I didn't know Hope very well," Katie said. "But I'm glad you do this for her. No one should die the way she did."

Faith paused for a moment. "Well, she did make that choice. It was her fault."

"Who knows what she was thinking that day?" Katie said. "Who knows what happened to her in school or on the way home that caused her to feel so lost and so alone that she made a choice that would change her life and the lives of all those who loved her?"

"She didn't want to die," Faith said. "She struggled."

"I'm sure she didn't," Katie said. "Once she realized what was happening, really happening, I'm sure she wanted to live. It must have been a horrible way to die."

"Well, let's go upstairs and we can talk about it more up there," Faith suggested.

Faith unlocked the house and the two women went upstairs.

"I've never been here," Katie said. "You had a lovely home."

"Yes, my mother insisted on the best," she replied. "And my mother always got what she wanted."

"She must have been devastated when Hope died," Katie said. "I can't even imagine what I'd do if one of my children died."

"My mother was fairly level-headed about the whole situation," Faith said. "She was the one to make all the arrangements so we could go back to being the perfect family once again."

"It would never be the same," Katie said. "No matter how hard you tried, it could never be the same."

They entered the bedroom and Katie saw there were two chairs in one corner of the room and a cord with a noose hanging down from the ceiling fan.

"This is where it happened," Faith said. "I hope it doesn't bother you that I hung up the cord. It helps me to remember the tragedy."

"Well, it's a little weird," Katie admitted. "But if that's what you need..."

Faith took Katie by the hand and pulled her over to the chairs. "Let's sit down and start the service," she said. "I'll say something about Hope and then you repeat it, like a chant. Okay?"

Katie was beginning to feel very uncomfortable about the whole situation. But the sooner she did what Faith wanted, the sooner she could go home. "Sure, that sounds good."

Faith jumped up and walked over to the noose. She hung a strand of crystals from it and lifted one end and let them go so they were slowly rocking back and forth. "We should watch the crystals," she said, "because they will remind us of Hope, so clear and pure."

Katie nodded and turned to the crystals.

"Hope is missed," Faith said.

"Hope is missed," Katie repeated.

"Hope is loved," Faith said.

"Hope is loved," Katie repeated.

"Hope is pure," Faith said.

"Hope is pure," Katie repeated.

Faith continued, often repeating other key phrases and having Katie repeat them over and over again. Katie found herself losing focus in the crystals and nearly falling asleep several times. She jerked herself back to attention and continued to repeat the phrases Faith was slowly, rhythmically saying. Finally, the crystals faded to black and Katie fell asleep.

Slipping from her chair, Faith walked over to Katie. She smiled as Katie softly snored, her head bent forward in slumber. "Katie," she whispered, "I want you to listen to me. Don't wake up, just listen. Okay?"

Katie nodded.

"Good. That's perfect," she said. "Just before she died, Hope whispered a name. The name of the person who killed her. Are you listening Katie?"

Katie nodded again.

"Just before she died, Hope said your name," Faith said.

Katie shook her head.

"Yes, she said Katie," Faith insisted. "You killed her. You killed my sister."

"No," Katie slurred.

"Yes, Katie," Faith said. "You killed Faith...I mean Hope...and now you need to kill yourself."

"My children," Katie whispered.

"Do you think they deserve a mother who is a killer?" Faith asked. "They deserve better."

"No, I didn't do it," Katie protested, her eyes still closed.

"You need to die, Katie," Faith said.

Tears rolled down Katie's cheeks. "I can't die," she said. "My children."

"Don't worry, Katie," Faith said. "I'll have someone help you, so it will be easier."

Faith stepped away from the chairs and opened the door to the hallway. "Come in," she invited.

Nick walked through the door and stopped in front of Faith.

"Nick, Katie killed Hope," Faith said. "I need you to put that noose around her neck and then pull her up toward the ceiling. Do you understand?"

Nick nodded. "Katie killed Hope," he repeated.

"Yes, so you need to put the noose around Katie's neck," Faith repeated. "Then walk over to the closet door and pull on the cord until Katie is up in the air and not breathing any more. Hope would want that."

Nick smiled. "Hope would want that."

"And then she will forgive you for kissing me," she repeated.

"I'm so sorry, Hope," he said. "I didn't mean to kiss Faith."

"And once you're done you need to jump out this window," Faith said, walking to the window and opening it up. "Then Hope will finally be at peace."

Chapter Forty-nine

Mary pulled the Roadster into the Brennan driveway, just behind Katie's van. "Oh, good, at least she hasn't left her house," Mary yelled, as she and Ian dashed toward the door.

Ian pounded on the front door. "Katie, it's Ian," he shouted. "Open the door."

He pounded again. "Katie, open the door."

"She has to be home," Mary said. "She promised me she'd stay home or call."

Ian ran across the porch and peered into the window. "The house looks empty," he said. "Are you sure you didn't miss any calls when you were inside the nursing home?"

Mary checked her phone. "Crap, I got a text," she said. "I never look at texts."

She read the text aloud. "They're at the house," she said, running down the stairs toward the car. "I'll drive and you call Bradley for backup."

Moments later, the Roadster spun out of the driveway and headed toward the highway.

"Bradley, it's Ian," he said once Bradley had answered. "Faith has Katie at her old house. Katie's in trouble. Send backup. We're on our way there."

"We're only a few minutes away," Mary said.

"Let's pray that's soon enough," Ian said.

He took Mary's phone and dialed a number.

"What are you doing?" she asked.

"Calling Katie," he said.

"Do you really think she has her phone?" Mary asked.

"Aye, I'm sure of it," he said. "At the funeral I took her aside and gave her a post-hypnotic suggestion that she was always to have her phone on her person if she left the house."

"But what if she's already hypnotized?" Mary asked.

"Well, I gave her a secondary suggestion," Ian said, "I told her the phone's ring will wake her from any trance."

Mary shook her head. "How did you know?"

He shrugged. "If it wasn't suicide, it had to be hypnosis," he said. "Hypnosis that led to death."

Chapter Fifty

The phone in Katie's pocket began to ring and she opened her eyes to find Nick standing in front of her. "What the…?" she began when Nick placed the noose over her head.

"You have to die because you killed Hope," Nick said pleasantly.

"Like hell I do," Katie said, lifting both of her feet and kicking Nick in the groin, sending him staggering back into the room, screaming in pain.

Katie slipped the noose off her neck and stood up, shaking the weariness from her. She glanced out the window and saw Faith exiting the house. But Nick's screams were loud enough to reach Faith's ears. She turned, looked up and saw Katie.

Running to her car, Faith pulled a handgun from the glove compartment and rushed back into the house. "Katie," she yelled, from the front hall. "Katie, it's your fault and you have to die."

She jogged up the stairs, arms outstretched with the gun ready to be fired. The door to the bedroom stood open. Nick was on the floor, clutching himself and still squealing like a stuck pig.

"Shut up you wimp," Faith screamed. "Where is she? Where is Katie?"

"I can't breathe," Nick screamed. "She wounded me permanently."

"If you couldn't breathe, you wouldn't be talking," Faith said. "So shut up."

Suddenly the door slammed and Faith whipped around.

"Katie," Faith screamed. "I know you're behind the door."

She shot her gun through the closed door, unloading the clip into the wood.

Behind her, the fan started to spin and the cord began to twirl around the room. Suddenly the window slammed shut behind her and Faith jumped.

"What the...?" she asked, turning to the window.

The room began to get colder and Faith could see her breath. "What's going on?" she demanded, her voice shaking. "What the hell is going on?"

"I'm sorry, Hope."

The familiar voice came from behind her. She turned slowly, not wanting to face what she knew she was going to see.

Faith's ghost stood underneath the fan, her face mottled and purple, her lips blue and her eyes bulging.

"You're dead," Hope whispered.

The ghost shook her head. "No, you're dead," she cried. "I'm sorry, Hope."

"I killed you," Hope cried.

"No, you didn't," the ghost replied. "I died because I deserved to die."

Hope shook her head and dropped the gun on the floor. "No, I wanted to die," she said. "I should have died that night. No one ever wanted me."

She climbed onto the chair and caught hold of the cord. "I want to be with you," she pleaded.

She placed the cord around her neck and turned to her sister. "Please."

The fan fell from the ceiling and the blades shattered from the force. The cord hung, harmlessly, from Hope's neck.

"You will be with me someday," Faith said. "But today is not the day."

Bradley pushed the door open, his gun drawn. "Put your hands in the air, where I can see them," he demanded.

Hope slowly lifted her hands and stepped down from the chair. "I killed them," she said. "I killed them all."

Chapter Fifty-one

Mary looked out of the bedroom window to the scene below. A police car drove down the driveway with Hope in the backseat, her face averted from the small group of people assembled in front of the house. Katie, sitting in the backseat of an open police car, was being questioned by a young officer.

Mary bit back a smile as she watched the ambulance pull away from the curb. Nick, the sole passenger, was still screaming about his injuries. And finally, Bradley was speaking with Mr. Foley, and by the look on the older man's face, it was not a pleasant conversation.

Mary turned away from the window and back to the bedroom. The fan lay on its side, the wooden blades broken into small pieces and a gaping hole in the ceiling. The cord was still attached to the doorknob and the fan, awaiting the forensics team to collect it as evidence. She slowly walked around the room and finally sat in the chair Katie had occupied. "Faith, are you still here?" she asked.

The temperature of the room dipped slightly and the ghost appeared before her. "Thank you," she whispered, "for saving Hope."

"I think you were the one who saved her," Mary said, looking pointedly at the fan on the ground.

"No, you stopped her," Faith said. "That's what saved her."

"Are you done here now?" Mary asked. "Can you cross over?"

Faith nodded. "I'm finally at peace."

She slowly faded away and the temperature in the room went back to normal.

Mary pulled out her cell phone and dialed a number. "Hello, Faye, this is Mary O'Reilly. You no longer have a ghost in your home. And once the police are finished with their investigation, you can move back in."

She smiled as the woman stammered on the other end.

"You have a nice day, Faye," she said. "I'll send you my invoice in the morning."

Chapter Fifty-two

"I can't believe it took us all day to find flower-girl dresses," Katie said, as she drove her van down their street.

"But they are the perfect dresses," Mary said, looking back at the two girls sound asleep in the back seat. "And we wore both of them out."

Katie laughed as she pulled into Mary's driveway and shifted into park. "Well, if I hadn't been driving I'd be napping too."

"How are you doing?" Mary asked.

Taking a deep breath, Katie glanced in her rearview mirror just to be sure the girls were asleep before she spoke. "I don't know which bothers me more," she admitted. "Waking up with some strange man trying to put a noose over my head or learning what actually happened to Hope. How could parents put their child through something like that?"

"I don't understand it either," Mary said. "You would think a parent's first instinct would be to protect and defend their child."

"Well, thank you for coming to the rescue," Katie said, reaching over and placing her hand on Mary's arm. "Bradley arrived just in the nick of time. I don't know how long I could have lain hidden in the bathtub."

"That was an excellent place to hide," Mary said. "Besides, it was your text that saved the day."

"I just have one question," Katie said. "Before Bradley came up, when Hope was coming after me, how did you get the bedroom door to slam?"

"Slam?" Mary asked.

"Yeah, the door slammed shut and Hope shot it full of holes," Katie said. "It was the perfect diversion."

"Katie, Ian and I drove in after Bradley," Mary said. "We watched him run into the house."

"But someone slammed the door and saved me," she said.

"Well, maybe Faith was a better friend than you thought," Mary replied.

Katie exhaled nervously. "Okay, well then, I think I better get home."

"Are you okay?" Mary asked.

She hesitated for a moment and then nodded. "Actually, I'm good. And I'm grateful to have you as a friend. Thank you."

She leaned forward and gave Mary a hug.

"You're welcome," Mary said. "And the feeling's mutual."

Mary got out of the van and opened the back door. "Hey, sleepyhead," she said to Clarissa. "We're home. Want to show your dad your new dress?"

"Uh-huh," she yawned, slowly unbuckling her seatbelt. "And my new shoes?"

"And your new shoes," Mary said.

Picking up several shopping bags and putting them in one hand, Mary placed her arm around Clarissa's shoulders and guided her out of the van. "Thanks for driving, Katie," she said.

"Thanks for buying the dresses," Katie replied. "Have a great night."

Mary pulled the back door shut and then guided Clarissa up the steps and into the house. Mary closed the door behind them, but they both stopped as soon as they walked into the house. "Something smells funny," Clarissa said, as she slipped off her coat.

"I agree," Mary said. "And it's coming from upstairs."

"Is it Uncle Ian?" Clarissa asked.

"No, he's at Nick's house, getting rid of the post-hypnotic suggestion," Mary said. "I suppose we should just go upstairs and see."

They climbed the stairs and found the second-floor hallway filled with furniture and drop cloths. Climbing around the items, they made their way toward Clarissa's room. The door was wide open and they both stopped and smiled when they saw what was waiting for them.

Bradley was standing in the far corner of the room wearing faded, torn, snug blue jeans and an old sleeveless t-shirt, that were splotched with fresh pink paint. He was putting a final coat of paint on the wall with a roller and was dancing along with the Rolling Stones as he painted.

Mary's heart skipped a beat at the way the muscles in his back rippled as he bent down and then reached up with the roller's long handle.

"Pull your tongue back in your mouth," Mike whispered. "There are children in the room."

Mary blushed. "Shhhh," she replied. "Can't you see I'm in lust?"

He chuckled. "Well, Captain Wonderful showed up about three minutes after you left," he said. "So he must have been watching and planning. He's been at this all day. I think he wanted to surprise both of you."

"Well, maybe we can sneak back down..."

"It's pink!" Clarissa yelled.

Bradley spun around, roller extended like a gun.

"Whoa there," Mike said. "That thing's loaded."

"I love my room," Clarissa said, hopping from drop cloth to drop cloth to reach Bradley. "It's the best room ever."

She wrapped her arms around him and hugged him tightly. "Thank you," she said.

Mary followed Clarissa. "It's beautiful," she said. "What a lovely surprise."

"Do you really think she likes it?" he asked.

"Look Mary, look! My bathroom's pink too!"

Mary smiled. "Oh, yes, I think this is definitely a winner."

She lay her hand on his chest, rubbing against the tautly-stretched cotton tee. "And do me a favor and keep this outfit," she said, with a soft sigh. "Suddenly pink-splattered shirts are even more appealing than black spandex ones."

He bent his head and caught her lips with his. "I'll have it bronzed," he said.

She shook her head. "Oh, no, you really need to wear it...often."

He grinned and was about to kiss her again when the doorbell rang.

She sighed. "I'll get it," she said. "You finish up in here."

She gave him one more quick kiss and made her way through the cluttered hallway to the staircase. She jogged down the stairs and was surprised to find the front door wide open.

"I'm sure I closed the door," she said aloud, instinctively slowing her pace and carefully studying the room.

Her heart accelerated as her first thought turned to Gary Copper, and, she decided immediately, there was no way he was going to get past her and up the stairs to Bradley or Clarissa. She slid up against the wall and made her way to the closet where she stored her gun. Reaching up to the top shelf and punching in the security code, she retrieved the firearm.

Making her way carefully through each room downstairs, she made sure everything was secure. Finally, she walked over to the door and peered outside. No one was on the porch and she couldn't see anyone up or down the street. She closed the door and slipped the deadbolt back in place, her heart rate slowing considerably.

"Well, stranger things have happened in this house," she said with a sigh of relief.

Turning to put her gun back in the safe, she saw a card sitting on top of the shopping bags she had just carried in. She walked over, picked up the card and gasped. *"Pleasant dreams, Mary,"* it read. *"Just remember, I'll be watching over you. Gary"*

About the author:

Terri Reid lives near Freeport, the home of the Mary O'Reilly Mystery Series, and loves a good ghost story. She lives in a hundred-year-old farmhouse complete with its own ghost. She loves hearing from her readers at author@terrireid.com.

Books by Terri Reid:

Loose Ends – A Mary O'Reilly Paranormal Mystery (Book One)

Good Tidings – A Mary O'Reilly Paranormal Mystery (Book Two)

Never Forgotten – A Mary O'Reilly Paranormal Mystery (Book Three)

Final Call – A Mary O'Reilly Paranormal Mystery (Book Four)

Darkness Exposed – A Mary O'Reilly Paranormal Mystery (Book Five)

Natural Reaction – A Mary O'Reilly Paranormal Mystery (Book Six)

Secret Hollows – A Mary O'Reilly Paranormal Mystery (Book Seven)

Broken Promises – A Mary O'Reilly Paranormal Mystery (Book Eight)

Twisted Paths – A Mary O'Reilly Paranormal Mystery (Book Nine)

Veiled Passages – A Mary O'Reilly Paranormal Mystery (Book Ten)

Bumpy Roads – A Mary O'Reilly Paranormal Mystery (Book Eleven)

The Ghosts Of New Orleans – A Paranormal Research and Containment Division (PRCD) Case File

Made in the USA
Lexington, KY
11 January 2015